GIRLS out late

ALSO AVAILABLE IN
DELL LAUREL-LEAF BOOKS

GIRLS *out late*

Book Three in the GIRLS Quartet

jacqueline wilson

LAUREL-LEAF BOOKS

Published by
Dell Laurel-Leaf
an imprint of
Random House Children's Books
a division of Random House, Inc.
New York

First American Edition 2002
First published in Great Britain by Doubleday, a division of Transworld Publishers Ltd, in 1999

Visit us on the Web! www.randomhouse.com/teens

Educators and librarians, for a variety of teaching tools, visit us at
www.randomhouse.com/teachers

ISBN: 0-440-22959-6

RL: 6.0

Reprinted by arrangement with Delacorte Press

Printed in the United States of America

June 2003

10 9 8 7 6 5 4 3 2 1

OPM

*To Meetal Malhi
and Harriet, Polina and Rebecca*

GIRLS *out late*

girl time

We're going out tonight, Nadine and Magda and me. It's not a Big Night Out. We're certainly not going to stay out late. We're just going on this little after-school shopping trip. No big deal at all. We'll meet at half past six at the Flowerfields Shopping Centre. Wander round the shops on their late night. We'll eat in McDonald's, then home by nine like good girls.

I don't bother to dress up or anything. I change out of my school uniform, obviously, but just into my black baggy trousers. They've been in the washing machine one spin too many times so that they're now technically not black at all, more a murky gray. Still, they're just about the only trousers in the whole world that are big without making me look enormous. They almost give the illusion that there's a weeny little bum and long lean legs hiding under all that bunchy material.

I try my newest stripy pink top but I'm not too sure about it now. It's a little too bright to be becoming. It makes my own cheeks glow positively peony. I wish I looked deathly pale and ethereal like my best friend Nadine. I'm stuck with permanently rosy cheeks—and *dimples*.

I search the airing cupboard for something dark and plain and end up purloining a dark gray V-necked school sweater belonging to my little brother, Eggs. It fits a little too snugly. I peer long and hard in my mirror, worrying about the prominence of my chest. No matter how I hunch up it still sticks out alarmingly. I'm not like my other best friend, Magda, who deliberately tightens the straps of her Wonder Bra until she can practically rest her chin on her chest. My own bras seem to be a bit too revealing. I try tucking a tissue in each cup so that I am not outlined too outrageously.

Then I attack my hair with a bristle brush, trying to tame it into submission. It's as if my entire body is trying to get out of control. My hair is the wildest of all. It's longish but so tightly curly it grows up and out as well as down. Nadine is so lucky. Her long licorice-black hair falls straight past her shoulders, no kinks at all. Magda's hair looks incredible, too, very short and stylish and bright red (dyed). It looks really great on her but if my hair was that short it would emphasize my chubby cheeks. Anyway, with my bright pink face I'd be mad to dye my hair scarlet. Not that my stepmum, Anna, would let me. She even gets a bit fussed when I use henna shampoo, for God's sake.

Anna eyes me now as I clatter into the kitchen to beg for some spare cash. Eggs is sitting at the table playing with the hands of my old alarm clock, muttering, "Four o'clock, telly time, fun. Five o'clock, more telly time, fun fun. Six o'clock, teatime, yum yum."

"That's my alarm clock," I say indignantly.

"But it's been broken for ages, Ellie. I thought it might help him learn the time. Do the big hand thing, Eggs," says Anna.

"Honestly, it's embarrassing having such a moron for a brother. And he was the one who broke it, fiddling around with the hands."

"Twelve o'clock, midnight, big sister turns into a pumpkin!" says Eggs, and shrieks with laughter.

"Are you off out, Ellie?"

"I'm just meeting Nadine and Magda to go late-night shopping."

"Seven o'clock, bathtime, splashy splashy. Eight o'clock, bedtime, yuck yuck."

"What about your homework?"

"I did it when I came home from school."

"No you didn't."

"I did, honestly."

"You were watching television."

"I did it *while* I was watching television."

I don't usually watch kids' TV but there's this new art program that has some amazingly cool ideas. I'm going to be a graphic artist when I grow up. I'm definitely not going to the art college where my dad lectures, though. I'm certainly not cut out to be one of his adoring students. It's weird to think that Anna was once. And my mum. She died when I was little but I still miss her a lot. Eggs isn't my whole brother, he's just a half.

"Thief!" Eggs suddenly screams, pointing at me. "That's my school jumper, take it *off*!"

"I'm just borrowing it for the evening."

He doesn't even like this school jumper. Anna has to sweet-talk him into it every morning. He prefers the weird, wacky, rainbow-colored concoctions that Anna knits for him. When he was going through his Teletubby phase he had four—purple, green, yellow and red—so he could be Tinky Winky, Dipsy, Laa-Laa or Po as the mood took him. Today Eggs is wearing his magenta Barney the Dinosaur jumper. I am immensely glad I am way past the stage of Anna making me natty knitted jumpers.

"But you'll muck it up," Eggs wails.

"*I'll* muck it up?"

Eggs is such a slurpy, splashy eater his clothes are permanently splattered orange (baked beans), yellow (egg yolk) and purple (Ribena). I examined his sweater for spots and stains very carefully indeed before putting it on.

"You'll make it smell."

"I won't! How dare you! I don't smell."

"You do, you do, doesn't she, Mum?" says Eggs.

"I *don't*," I say, but I'm starting to get panicky. I don't really smell, do I? Has my deodorant stopped working? Oh God, does everyone back away from me with wary expressions and pinched nostrils and I just haven't noticed?

"Ellie doesn't smell," says Anna.

"She does, of that yucky powdery sweet scenty stuff. I don't want my school sweater ponging like a girl," Eggs insists, tugging at the jumper. I swat his hands away as best I can.

"Stop him, Anna, he'll rip it!"

"Yes, give over, Eggs. Though it is *his* sweater. Honestly, for years and years you wore your dad's extra-large T-shirts that came way past your knees. Now you want to wear Eggs's teeny weeny little sweaters. When are you going to wear anything that fits?"

I don't ever borrow Anna's clothes. We have very different styles, even though she's only fourteen years older than me. And we're very different shapes, too. She's skinny, I'm not. But I've decided I'm not going to let that bug me anymore.

I went on a seriously intense diet last term and started to get obsessed about my weight. But now I'm getting back to normal.

To prove it I eat a toasted cheese sandwich with Anna and Eggs even though I'll be munching at McDonald's later.

"What time shall I get Dad to come and pick you up?" says Anna.

"I don't need Dad to pick me up, I'll get the bus back."

"Are you sure? I don't like the idea of you coming back on your own when it's getting dark."

"I won't *be* on my own. I'll be with Nadine all the way on the bus, and as far as Park Hill Road."

"Tell you what, you travel back to Nadine's house and give us a ring when you get back there. Then Dad can drive round and give you a lift, OK?"

"OK, OK."

I smile at Anna and she smiles back as we acknowledge our compromise. We never used to get on, but it's weird, now we're kind of friends.

"It's not OK. Tell her to give me back my school jumper, Mum!" Eggs yells, kicking at me.

I will never be friends with Eggs. He's still wearing his school lace-ups and he's really hurting my shins. I might be wearing combat trousers but they're totally ineffective against weapons of war.

"Don't get me all hot and bothered, Eggs, or I might have to go and spray myself with perfume to cool down," I say. "I *might* accidentally douse your dopey old sweater."

"No, no, no! Don't you dare!"

"Stop teasing him, Ellie," says Anna, sighing. She's digging in her handbag. "How much pocket money have you got left?"

"Absolutely zilch. In fact I owe Magda, she paid for me to go swimming last Sunday."

"And you already owe me for that pair of tights from Sock Shop."

"Oh God, yes. Help, I'm bound for the debtors' prison."

"Can't you kind of—budget?" says Anna, un-zipping her purse.

"I try, but Dad's such a meany. Magda gets twice what I get for her allowance."

"Don't start, Ellie."

"But it's not fair."

"*Life* isn't fair."

I'll say. Still, the minute I'm fourteen, I'm all set to get *some* kind of paid work—you name it, I'll do it—and then I'll be able to keep up with Magda and Nadine. Well, halfway up.

"Here you are." Anna hands me a fiver.

I feel a bit mean. Anna hasn't got a job either. She's been looking hard since Eggs started school but there's nothing going. She has to cadge cash from Dad too. Marriage certainly isn't fair. Catch me ever getting married. In fact I'm not too sure I want anything to do with boys at all.

Magda is totally boy-mad. Nadine isn't quite as crazy, although last year she went out with this total creep called Liam who treated her like dirt. I had a sort of boyfriend then too. Well, a boy who was a friend, rather than a *boy*friend. He certainly wasn't a dreamboat but he seemed to be dead keen on me. He wrote me all these love letters and couldn't wait to see me. He declared true love forever and ever. But then his letters fizzled out and it turned out he had met this other girl and now he's declared true love forever and ever to her. As if I care. She's welcome to him. I don't want him anymore. I don't want a boyfriend at all. Really.

So anyway, I rush round to Nadine's place and she is in the middle of an argument with her mum. She's mad at Nadine because she wants her to go to this line-dancing class with her and Natasha. It's a truly sad session where lots of mums go with their daughters. Nadine's mum is dead keen on line dancing and has made herself a denim skirt with matching waistcoat and she wears a pair of white fringed cowboy boots. Natasha adores her baby cowgirl outfit. She loves line dancing too and is already the little star of the class. Nadine's mum bought enough blue denim to make another matching set for Nadine. She would willingly pay for another pair of white cowgirl boots. Nadine would rather *die* than go line dancing in a blue denim outfit and white cowgirl boots—especially with her mum and her loathsome little sister.

"I sometimes feel you're not part of this family at all," says Nadine's mum.

"I sometimes wish I *wasn't* part of this family," Nadine says defiantly. "I'm going down to Flowerfields with Ellie."

"Flowerfields! What's the matter with you? Only this Saturday you made such a fuss because I wanted you to come shopping in the Flowerfields Centre with Natasha and me and what did you say? Only that you couldn't stick going shopping, *especially* in the Flowerfields Shopping Centre."

Nadine rolls her eyes, already extra expressive with their thick outline of black kohl.

Nadine's mum sighs. "Are you as insolent to your mother, Ellie?"

"Well, it's different," I say diplomatically. "I mean, Anna's my stepmother but she's more my age. We're more like sisters. It's not like she's really a mum figure."

"I wish I didn't have a mum figure," says

Nadine when we finally escape. "God, she doesn't half go on. And Natasha's driving me nuts too. Just think, I've got four or five more years before there's a chance of breaking free. How am I going to survive?" She clenches her fist dramatically, then wails, "Oh *bum*, my nail!"

Nadine spends the next five minutes mourning her broken nail. I eventually divert her by planning out our blissful life in the future when we're eighteen and have fully served our life sentences with our families. We'll both go to art college, me to do graphics, Nadine to do fashion. We'll get our own little flat. We'll get up when we want and eat when we want and go out when we want and hold a party every single Saturday.

We plan it all out on the bus into town and we're still busy negotiating over the interior decorating when we meet up with Magda at the Flowerfields entrance. We're momentarily diverted. Magda looks stunning in a skimpy little pink lacy top that shows off every single *pore*. My heart beats enviously under its pad of paper tissue. If only I had Magda's confidence!

"You've got that new top!"

"And new trousers," says Nadine, eyeing them up and down. She darts round Magda's back and pulls at the waistband. "Wow, DKNY! Where did you get them?"

"Oh, my auntie Cath came round at the weekend. She bought the trousers in Bond Street weeks ago, meaning to go on a diet to fit into them, but she hasn't lost a pound, so guess what, I got lucky."

"Why haven't I got a lovely auntie?" says Nadine. "Did she give you the top too?" She fingers it enviously with her one-tenth defective long nails.

"She bought it for me as a present, yeah. Do you like the color? You don't think it clashes with my hair?"

"Everything clashes with your hair," I say, ruffling her amazing crimson curls.

"I want to get a lipstick the same pearly pink," says Magda. "Come on, girls. *Shopping* time!"

We spend hours and hours and hours circling the makeup stands in Boots while Magda anoints her wrists with pink stripes in her attempt to find the perfect pink. Nadine is happy enough playing with makeup samples and experimenting with black lipstick and silver blusher but I get a bit fed up. I'm not really into makeup actually. I mean, I've got some and I shove it on if I'm going out anywhere special, but I always forget and dab my eyes and smear it or wipe my mouth and end up with lipstick on my chin.

Then we spend hours and hours and hours at the nail varnish stands. Nadine ends up buying a nail-lengthening kit, one of those fun sets where you can paint on false nails all different patterns and add little sequins and beads and stuff. Magda buys one too but I know I'd forget and nibble mine off. I'm going to stop biting my nails *one* day, but at the moment my teeth have a beaverlike will of their own and gnaw my fingers ferociously.

"Come on, you guys, the shops will be shutting soon," I moan—and eventually they let me drag them up to this art shop on the top floor. They get fed up after the first few seconds and hang around outside while I finger the fat white sketchpads and lust after the huge shiny tins of rainbow felt-tips. I'm only in there a minute but Magda and Nadine keep putting their heads round the door and yelling at me. I try out the pens, writing "I am Ellie and I like to draw." I do so, squiggling a little elephant with a wavy trunk with an 07 point and a weeny 03 point and a mean green and a flam-boyant pink and after *more* moans from outside I end up buying the 05 black pen I always choose and a little square black sketchbook that I simply can't resist. I haven't got too much money left. I'm going to have to beg a few chips off Magda and Nadine or go hungry—but I'm happy.

The three of us link arms and wander round the rest of the shops, trying on high heels in Office and staggering around like drunks, and then we spend ages in the HMV store listening to the latest Claudie Coleman album. Magda, Nadine and I have entirely different musical tastes but we are all united in our admiration for Claudie. Magda likes her because she sings songs with very powerful, positive lyrics. Nadine likes her because her music is very cool and hip. I like her because she's got long, wild curly hair a bit like mine but much lovelier and she's not a bit fat but she is much curvier than your average rock chick. So she's kind of my role model.

The HMV store is crowded. Magda automatically stands wherever there's a clump of likely-looking boys. They all stare at her appreciatively and three of them start chatting her up. Nadine and I sigh and slope off. This is a familiar situation and it sucks.

"Three boys, three girls, and all three want to be the one who gets Magda," says Nadine. She is too nice to point out that she is always second choice. It's easy enough to work out where I come—last!

"Hey, wait for me!" says Magda, scurrying after us. The boys call after her but she doesn't take any notice.

"You stay with them if you want," I say.

"Yeah, we're going down to McDonald's but you can catch up with us later," says Nadine.

"I'm catching up with you now," says Magda.

"This is our girl time, right? Hey, *look* at the time! It's getting late. Come on, let's eat."

Magda is sweet enough to insist on buying me a burger and fries. I draw her portrait on the first page of my sketchbook, picturing her doing a little twirl in her pink top and designer trousers with lots of adoring weeny guys milling around her ankles. Then I draw Nadine. First of all I tease her and kit her out in Rhinestone Cowboy gear, but after she's clobbered me I appease her by drawing her as a glamorous witch with nails like jeweled claws and in one elaborately manicured hand she's holding a little doll, the image of Natasha, stuck all over with pins.

I'm really into drawing now so I peer round for someone to sketch. And then I see the strangest thing. There's a boy the other side of McDonald's. *He's* not strange. He's quite good-looking with dark eyes and long, floppy hair. He's wearing a Halmer High School uniform. A lot of the boys who go there are either Hooray Henrys or the twitchy nerdy type. But this boy's different. Guess what he's doing! He's got a pen and a little notebook similar to mine and he's sketching . . . *me*?

It can't be me. No, of course, it's Magda. She's the one all the boys stare at all the time. But when he looks up he's staring straight at me—and when Magda goes to get another straw for her milk shake he doesn't turn his head. Then it'll be Nadine. Yes, he's drawing Nadine with her amazing long hair and big dark eyes. Though Nadine is lolling back in her chair and I'm not sure he can see her properly now.

It's me he's looking at. Looking up at my face and down at his book, up and down, up and down, his pen moving rapidly across the page. He must see I'm staring at him but it doesn't put him off.

"Why have you gone pink, Ellie?" says Nadine.

"Oh God, I haven't, have I?"

"Shocking pink. What *is* it?"

"Nothing."

"Who are you looking at?" says Magda, coming back with the straw. She peers round and susses things out straightaway. "Are you flirting with that Halmer High guy?"

"No."

"*Which* boy?" says Nadine, peering.

"Don't! He's staring at us."

"So we'll stare at him," says Magda. "What's he doing, writing?"

"I think he's sketching," I say.

"What?"

"Me!"

Magda and Nadine look at me. They both look a little surprised.

"What's he drawing you for?" says Nadine.

"*I* don't know. It feels . . . weird," I say, as his eyes flicker up and down again.

"So you draw him," says Magda. "Go on, Ellie."

"It'll look silly."

"No it won't. Go on. He's drawing you, so you draw him. Even-steven," says Magda.

"All right." I start sketching the sketcher. I try a jokey portrait, making his eyes extra-beady, his hair a little too long, his stance ultra-alert. I draw the sketchbook in his hand with a small picture of me. In this picture I am crouched over my own sketchbook, drawing a minute portrait of him.

"It's good!" says Magda.

"So you're drawing him drawing you drawing him . . . it's making my brain buzz thinking about it," says Nadine.

"Hey, he's coming over!" says Magda.

"What?" I say, looking up. She's right, he's walking our way, still staring at me.

I shut my sketchbook up quickly and slide it onto my lap.

"Hey, that's not fair. I want to see what you've drawn," he says, standing at our table. He smiles at me. "I'll show you mine if you show me yours."

Magda and Nadine burst out laughing.

"That's an invitation you can't resist, Ellie," says Magda.

"Ellie! Hey, you're not Ellie the Elephant, are you?" he says.

I stare at him. Ellie . . . the Elephant? Why is he calling me my old nickname? Does he think I'm that fat?

All my old anorexic loopiness overwhelms me. I feel like I'm being blown up like a balloon. Roll up, roll up to peer at the fat lady in McDonald's.

"Ellie the Elephant?" I whisper in a mouse's squeak out of my gargantuan head.

"Yes, I was in the art shop upstairs just now, you know?"

"Does she know?" says Magda. "She only spends half her life there."

"Half *our* lives," says Nadine.

"Me too, me too," he says. "Anyway, I was buying this new pen and I went to try it out and someone else had been writing all across the pad, and there was this name, Ellie, and a cute little elephant with a wavy trunk."

"Oh! Yes, I *see*. That was me," I say, shrinking back into my ordinary-size self.

"So have you been drawing lots of little elephants, eh?"

"I hope not," says Magda. "Seeing as she's supposed to have been drawing me."

"And me," says Nadine. "And also you!"

"Me?" he says eagerly.

"Shut up, Nadine," I say.

"Oh come on, let me see. Look." He opens his own sketchbook. "Here's you."

I peer at it, my heart thudding. I've never seen my portrait drawn by anyone else. Well, I suppose Eggs has included me in his shaky crayonings of MY FAMILY, but as he represents me as two big blobs, four stick lines and a wild scribble of hair, his portraits are not very flattering.

This boy's portrait of me is . . . amazing. He's brilliant at art. His pen is the same as mine and yet he's got it to swoop and spiral with such style. He's obviously a fan of Aubrey Beardsley. He places his figure on the paper with that kind of confidence, a bold outline, and immense detail with the hair, the features and the texture of the jumper. My hair, my features, my jumper (well, on loan from Eggs). He's drawn me looking the way I'd *like* to look, intelligent and absorbed, drawing in my own sketchbook. Drawing him. And the picture of me is drawing a minute portrait too.

"Wow!" says Nadine. "Look, he's drawn you drawing him drawing you and you've drawn him drawing you drawing him."

"You're burbling, Nadine," says Magda. "Here, Ellie, show him."

She snatches my sketchbook and shows him my portrait of him. He laughs delightedly.

"It's great."

"It's *not,* nowhere near as good as yours."

It's annoying, I'm not really desperately competitive, and I couldn't care less about coming top at school or winning at games and stuff like that, but the one thing I suppose I've always taken for granted is that I'm good at art. Better than anyone else in my class.

"What year are you in?" I ask.

"Year Eleven."

It makes it a little easier. Maybe in two years' time I'll be as good as that. Maybe.

"What year are you in, Ellie?"

"Year Nine, we all are."

Nadine raises her eyebrows at Magda, and they both sigh, irritated at me for giving away our age. I suppose they could both get away with making out they were Year Ten. Maybe even older. But I'm smaller than them and with my chubby cheeks and dimples I could easily be mistaken for some little kid of eleven or twelve. Apart from my chest. I wriggle in my chair. I'm *not* sticking my chest out. I'm just sitting up a little straighter.

"I'm going to get myself another coffee, can I get you girls anything?"

"Well, we were just going," I say.

"No we weren't," says Magda. "Sure, coffee would be great."

He smiles and goes off to the counter, leaving his sketchbook on the table.

"I haven't got any more money," I whisper. "I already owe you, Mags."

"He can pay. He'll have stacks of cash seeing he's a poshnob Halmer's boy," says Nadine. "He really fancies you, Ellie."

"No he doesn't!" I say quickly, blushing again. "He's just being friendly, that's all."

"Oh yeah, like he trots round the whole of McDonald's buying everyone coffee?"

"It was just because I was drawing. Anyway, it's probably not me he's interested in. It could be you he fancies, Nadine—or Magda."

"Do you think so?" says Magda, twiddling her hair and licking her lips.

"You wish, Mags," says Nadine. "He's only got eyes for Ellie."

He comes back with the coffee and then he sits down beside us. Beside me.

"So what else have you been drawing, Ellie? I'm Russell, by the way."

He holds out his hand. I blink at him. I think he's being incredibly formal and wants to shake my hand. He looks surprised when I hold out my own hand politely.

"I was reaching for your sketchbook, actually."

"Oh!" I feel myself blushing scarlet and try to snatch my hand away.

"Let's shake anyway. That makes us friends," says Russell, giving my hand a little squeeze.

Nadine gives Magda a triumphant nod. She's right. I can't believe it. I feel like I'm suddenly rocketed onto Romance Planet. Things like this don't happen to me.

"Let's see the sketchbook," he says. He looks at my jokey portraits of Magda and Nadine.

"They're really fantastic," he says, grinning.

"No they're not. They were just quick sketches anyway. I can draw a bit better than that," I say. "But I'm nowhere near as good as you."

"No, I think you've got a real gift, Ellie. Do you want to do graphics later?"

He's treating me like a serious person. *He's* a serious person. The only boyfriend I've ever had thought that you spelt it *graffix* and reckoned it was a stick of glue.

"Yeah, maybe," I said casually.

"There's supposed to be a very good graphics course at Kingtown Art College," says Russell.

"I don't really fancy going there. It's where my dad teaches," I say.

"Oh, right. I know the problem. My mum teaches in the juniors at my school and it was seriously weird putting my hand up and calling her Miss. I rather hoped she might make me teacher's pet and top of the class but she kept picking on me."

We get launched into this whole long conversation about schools. Magda says something about her embarrassing enormous packed lunches when she was at junior school. Her mum and dad run a restaurant and if they are fond of anyone they want to feed them up. They're very, very, very fond of Magda. Most people are. But Russell hardly seems to notice her, though he nods politely. Magda gives up.

"Shall we buzz off home, Nadine?" she suggests.

"Good idea," Nadine says. "Bye, Ellie, see you tomorrow."

"No, wait, I'm coming too," I say.

"Can I come as well?" says Russell. "Which way home do you go, Ellie?"

"I go on the bus with Nadine."

"Oh, that's great, so do I," says Russell.

"You don't even know which bus."

"Your bus."

Magda and Nadine roll their eyes. I giggle stupidly. I feel my cheeks with the back of my hand. They're hot enough to fry a couple of eggs. At least

I cool down a little outside. Magda waves goodbye and goes off shaking her head, still a little bemused. I trot along awkwardly between Russell and Nadine, trying like mad to think of something intelligent to talk about. I want to ask Russell all sorts of stuff about art but I don't want to leave Nadine out of things. Yet if I start chattering to Nadine about French homework and what combination of colors she is going to paint her nails then it'll seem rude to Russell.

I glance nervously from one to the other. Both of them catch me looking. Nadine rolls her eyes at me. Russell smiles. He clears his throat. He hums a little tune. Perhaps he is lost for words too. This is surprisingly reassuring.

"Have you got their latest album?" says Nadine.

I stare at her blankly but Russell responds. He was humming this song by some cult hip band Nadine is nuts on. I've never even heard of them. Russell and Nadine burble on about them.

"What do you think of Animal Angst, Ellie?" Russell asks.

I blink at him. I wouldn't know Animal Angst if it howled in my ear. "Oh, OK," I say cautiously.

Nadine gives her eyes another roll, but she doesn't betray me. I resolve to read the *New Musical Express* every week.

We stand waiting for the bus. There's a big poster for a horror movie over the road. *Girls Out Even Later.*

"Great," says Russell. "It's coming out on Friday. The gory special effects are meant to be superb. Did you want to see it, Ellie?"

I dither helplessly. Does he mean—do I want to see it *with him*?

I want to go out with him, yes please! But I hate horror movies. I have to hide my eyes at all the scary parts. I can't even listen to creepy music or I come out in goose pimples. I've only ever seen horror movies on video. It would be much much scarier on a huge screen. I'd probably make a right idiot of myself with Russell and end up cowering right under the seat. If I ever got *in* as it's an eighteen. I haven't got a hope in hell of convincing anyone that I'm eighteen.

Russell is looking at me, waiting for a reply.

"Mmmmm," I say eventually, fully aware that this reply is not worth the wait.

Nadine launches into a long rave about the director's last horror movie. I stand and stare into the middle distance. Russell seems fascinated. He's obviously realizing that he has been hitting on the wrong girl. He and Nadine are soul mates.

"What did you think of *Girls Out Late,* Ellie?" he asks.

"OK," I mumble.

"Did you like it?" Russell presses me.

"Mmmm."

I seem to have taken to talking in initials: *O, K* and *M.*

"Did you like the creepy bit in the multistory car park?" says Russell.

I look at Nadine for help.

This time she betrays me by bursting out laughing. "Ellie never got that far," she says. "She started to watch it round at my place but had to hide her eyes before the title sequence was over. She only got ten minutes into the movie proper before running right out of my bedroom and refusing to come back."

Russell grins. "So you find horror movies a bit scary, Ellie?"

"Ellie's the type of girl who'd find the Noo-Noo scary," Nadine giggles.

My face is certainly Po red. Russell must take me for a right idiot. He's laughing at me.

"Then *please* come to the movie with me, Ellie—you'll be snuggling right up to me in no time," he says.

I manage to laugh too, though I still feel a bit foolish. I glance at my watch. Talk about girls out late! It's nearly ten.

Still, the bus is coming, I'll be home soon. At least, that's what I *intend.*

time to go home

I don't know who to sit next to on the bus. Nadine gets on first and rather pointedly spreads herself out on a double seat. I make for the seat opposite but I suddenly feel mean. Nadine's been my best friend since we were both five years old. I've known Russell less than an hour, for God's sake. I spin on my heel and nudge up next to Nadine. Russell sits opposite. He leans forward to try to continue the conversation but this old lady huffs and puffs so he contents himself with smiling.

Nadine and I can converse OK.

"Gee whiz, I thought Magda was a quick worker!" Nadine mutters. "I've obviously underestimated your pulling power, Ellie."

"It's nothing to do with me!" I whisper.

"Rubbish, it was all your come-hither looks, staring at him all the time in McDonald's."

"I was drawing him! I had to look at him. And, anyway, he drew me first. He was the one who started it."

"So, what happens now? Are you going to go out with him?"

"I don't know. I don't think he'll ask me. He was just being friendly because of the art thing."

"*Ellie!* Are you being deliberately irritating? He's obviously nuts about you."

"Do you really think so?" I whisper, delighted.

Nadine sighs. "Look, when I get off the bus I'll clear off down Weston Avenue and go that way home, OK? I don't want to play gooseberry."

"You're not!"

"Oh, yeah, well, I'm not going to stand and file my broken fingernails while you stand snogging on the doorstep."

"I'm not going to snog!" I forget to whisper. Nadine nudges me. Russell is staring at me. Oh God, did he hear what I said?

"Of course you'll snog," says Nadine.

"I don't think I want to."

"Don't you fancy him?"

"I . . . don't know," I say stupidly. "What do *you* think of him, Nad?"

"Well, he's OK. I mean he's not really my type."

"Do you think he's good-looking?"

"Sort of. Well, he's not totally nerdy, but it's hard to tell when he's wearing that awful uniform."

"Nadine, when you snog—like now, first time—are you supposed to do the tongue thing?"

"If you want to."

"I don't know *what* I want."

It's true. I always dreamt of a romantic encounter like this—and yet now it is happening it's so overwhelming I'm kind of scared. I almost wish Russell had gone after Magda or Nadine. No, I don't really wish that. I wish Russell had never started sketching me, and that now I was going home on the bus with Nadine after a perfectly normal girls' night out.

"Come on, it's our stop," says Nadine.

"Maybe he'll stay on the bus," I say.

"You're mad, Ellie. Look, he's getting up too."

"Nadine, don't go down Weston Avenue. Come my way. Come via my house. *Please,* I don't want to be on my own with him," I whisper urgently.

"Grow up, Ellie!"

That's the trouble, I'm not sure I want to grow up.

We get off the bus, Russell, Nadine and me.

"Well, cheerio, you guys," says Nadine.

"Nadine!"

"See you tomorrow, Ellie." She nods at Russell.

"Bye, Nadine, nice meeting you," says Russell. Then he turns to me. "Which way do we go?"

"We can go Nadine's way," I say.

But Nadine is already running off, clonking a little in her new Shelley's shoes.

"We'll go your way," says Russell. "Or there-abouts. Shall we go for a little walk first?"

"Well . . ." I've got matching silver bangles jangling on my wrist instead of my watch—but I know it's getting late. Not just getting. It *is* late. I am a Girl Out Late. I've got to get home. He can walk me to my door and then I will give him a quick little kiss on the cheek and then I'll scoot indoors. That's what I'll do. That's what I want.

It's not what he wants.

"Come on, Ellie!" He's looking all around. "Is there a park round here? Come and show me so that I can imagine a chubby little Ellie feeding the ducks."

"No duck pond, no ducks. Swings."

"Swings are better. A little swing in the park for five minutes. Ten at tops. Yes?"

My head nods automatically. We walk toward the park. Russell edges nearer to me. He reaches out. He takes hold of my hand.

Oh God, I don't know what to do with my fingers. They're crooked uncomfortably but if I fold them over they may stroke his palm in a suggestive way. My hand starts sweating, or is it *his*? If only it was the bitter cold winter and then we'd be wearing gloves.

But it's spring and I'm getting uncomfortably hot inside Eggs's tight sweater. What am I doing? I want to go *home,* and it really is late. I'm going to get into trouble.

"I'll have to get back soon, Russell, really."

"Sure, well, so will I."

"Where do you live?"

"Oh, around here."

"No you don't, not if you don't even know where the park is!"

"It's . . . over there." He gestures vaguely with his free hand.

"Totally wrong. Come on, where do you live specifically?"

"Near the park."

"Lies!"

"OK, near *a* park, Pembridge Park."

"That's *miles* away!"

It's also the posh part of town, with huge great Victorian houses. I once went to a party there and I remember being astonished by the stained-glass windows in the hall—I went into the living room expecting pews and an altar. Some of the grandest houses surrounding the park certainly seem as big as churches and induce a similar feeling of reverence. And I'm hand in hand with a Halmer's boy who lives there.

"A big house?" I say.

"It is, but we just have a basement flat. Well, it's called a garden flat but the garden is outside and we only have a fifth of it. The house is all split up. So are my family. I live with my dad now and my sister lives with my mum. There is also my dad's girlfriend, but the less said about her the better. I hope she fades out of the picture soon. I certainly don't fancy her as a stepmother."

"I've got a stepmother. She's OK, though. We didn't used to get on but now we're friends."

Anna won't be friends anymore unless I go home *now*. She'll worry.

"I'm never ever going to be friends with Cynthia. Honestly, what a classic name—my stupid besotted dad is sinning with Cynthia. I don't know what's up with him. We used to get on great, Dad and me, sort of us two guys together—but now she's there all the time. It's pathetic. So I try not to hang out too much at home now. Who wants to be cooped up in the living room with his dad and his dad's girl snogging on the sofa like teenagers?"

"In front of you? That's a bit gross."

"Well, whenever I go out of the room. Then they spring apart when I go back in. It's like I'm the parent. So I mostly clear off to my bedroom, draw and do homework and stuff. But sometimes it really gets to me, stuck there like someone in solitary confinement—so I push off by myself."

"Don't you have any friends?"

"Oh, yes, heaps. No, don't get the impression I'm this poor sad guy without a social life."

"I didn't mean that!"

"It's just, well, I'm OK at school, there's this little mob I go around with. But out of school—well, there's two types at Halmer's, there's the really intense anoraks and they just swot away and come top in everything and their idea of a big social thrill is accessing some porn on the Internet. Then there's the other really hip set, the ones that go to all the parties and get all the girls and drink and take drugs—and I'm a bit too wet and weedy to join in."

"You're not a bit wet or weedy," I say.

"But it's kind of different for boys anyway. You have mates, but you're not really *close* to them. Unless you're gay, which I'm definitely not, in spite of all the tales you hear of infamous encounters behind the Halmer's bike sheds."

I giggle. Magda was once chatted up by this Halmer's boy in Year Eight and he swore half the Year Elevens were at it—behind the bike sheds.

"It must be great to have friends to go round with, like you and those two girls."

"Nadine and Magda. Yeah, they're both my best friends."

"Which do you like best?"

"Both."

"You don't ever fall out?"

"Well, we have arguments sometimes. And last year Nadine had this ultra-creepy boyfriend so we didn't see much of her then—but we're like this now." I cross my fingers on my free hand.

We are still clasped, albeit a little sweatily. We're nearly at the park now. A minute or two, then maybe one quick swing and then *home*.

"Does Nadine have a boyfriend now?"

"No."

"I bet the other one does, the bubbly one with the red hair."

"Magda? No, she doesn't have a boyfriend either."

"And what about you, Ellie?"

I pause. I shake my head.

Russell smiles. "Great, so . . . will you come out with me sometime?"

"I *am* out with you."

"No, I mean for a pizza or to see a film or something."

"OK."

"Tomorrow?"

"If you like."

"Seven o'clock. I could meet you at that shopping center place. I'll be the guy sketching in case you forget what I look like."

"Yeah, so I had better be going home now. It's ever so late."

"No, it's not, look, some of the kids are still out playing."

There's a little bunch of them whizzing around on the roundabout in the dark, sharing crisps and swigging Coke.

"Well, I know it's not *late*-late but I was supposed to be home ages ago."

"But we haven't had a swing yet. Come on, Ellie. One quick swing."

"OK, one quintessentially quick swing and then I must *go home*."

"Promise. I love the way you talk, Ellie. You're so different from other girls."

We walk over the tufty grass toward the play area. I'm glad I'm not wearing my high heels. I'm wearing shabby red trainers, the rubber treads worn right down—but I feel I'm bouncing on springs. It's really happening. I'm Ellie and I'm walking hand in hand with this boy who likes it that I'm different. He likes *me,* he likes *me,* he likes *me*.

We get to the swings and I think of all the times I've been here in the past. First with my mum, and there's a sad little tug of my heart even now because I still miss her so much and she'll *always* come first with me. Then there were the times Dad took me, pushing me so high on the swings I'd get scared I'd loop the loop right over the bar at the top. Nowadays Dad pushes Eggs, who once fell right off and nearly lived up to his nickname and scrambled himself. Magda, Nadine and I sometimes hang out in the park in the summer too and have long long long discussions about clothes and makeup and hairstyles and rock stars and *boys*.

And now I'm here with a boy, and he's swinging and I'm swinging, kicking right up high until my trainers point higher than the tops of the silhouetted poplars edging the park. I put my head back and make it feel even speedier but I start to get giddy and when I slow down and jump off, the park suddenly tips sideways and spins by itself.

"Whoops," says Russell, and he reaches out and steadies me. "Are you OK, Ellie?"

Then before I can answer he bends his head and kisses me. It's just a little kiss, our lips gently bumping. We break away. I blink behind my bleary glasses.

"Oh, Ellie," says Russell, and he kisses me again. A proper kiss. A real pressed-up-close, mouths working, meaningful kiss. I never thought it would feel so strange, so special. I feel even giddier. I cling to him and he holds me even closer.

There's something spraying in my hair. Is it

raining? And little flaky things land on my shoulder. *Snowing?*

Laughter.

I push Russell away. The kids are surrounding us, deliberately sprinkling us with Coke and crisps.

"Snog snog snoggy snog!" they jeer.

"Get lost, you lot," says Russell.

He has a crisp sticking up in his hair like a little ribbon. I remove it—and we both start giggling.

"Let's find somewhere a bit more private," says Russell, taking my hand. "Over by the trees?"

"No, I must get back, really."

"Oh, come on—please, Ellie."

"I'm sure it's time to go home."

"Like Andy Pandy. Did you ever see that *Watch with Mother* video? I love little kids' programs."

"Me too! I used to like *Sesame Street* best."

"And me. I used to draw them all with my felt-tip pens. All my little buddies in the nursery class wanted one of my special Big Bird portraits."

"You'll have to draw the Cookie Monster for me, he's my favorite."

"Did you like *Art Attack* when Zoe Ball was on it, ages and ages ago?"

"Yes, I *loved* it."

"There's this guy in my class crazy about Zoe

Ball, and he paid me a fiver to do a special portrait of him with his arm round her."

"Hey, that's a great idea. All the girls in my class are nuts about Leonardo DiCaprio so maybe I'll do heaps of portraits of him and make my fortune."

"Some people say I look a bit like Leonardo DiCaprio—you know, my hairstyle and my features. Do you think so, Ellie?"

I mumble something politely. He doesn't look *remotely* like Leonardo DiCaprio. I'm glad Nadine and Magda aren't here or they'd hoot with laughter. We've left the kids on the swings far behind. We're over by the trees where it's really dark.

"Oh, Ellie," says Russell.

This is obviously a signal for another kiss. I'm ready this time, my head tilted so that my glasses don't get in the way. I love the way he kisses. Dan and I used to kiss but it was just silly awkward kids' stuff. This is real and adult and exciting.

This is getting too real and adult and exciting. His hand is wandering over my shoulders toward my front.

"Russell, don't."

"Please. Just . . . *please*."

His hand is stroking the wool of Eggs's jumper insistently. I love the way it feels. It's not like it's anything too terrible. I don't want him to think me totally uptight and pathetic. So shall I just let him go this far?

Oh my God, I've suddenly remembered the tissues! The ones I stuffed down each bra cup so I wouldn't show too much in the tight sweater. I'll die if he finds himself with a handful of paper tissue.

"Please, Russell. No, come on, I *have* to get home." I push him away very firmly.

"Ellie!"

"I mean it. What's the time?"

He looks at his watch. "Oh dear, I can't see the face in the dark."

"Russell, *please!*"

"OK, OK. It's only just gone eleven."

"*What?* You're kidding!"

"Ten past."

"Oh my God, what am I going to do?"

"Hey, hey, don't panic. Look, it's really not late at all. Ellie! Wait for me."

"I've got to run."

"Well, I'll run with you. I'll take you right home. I'll explain to your folks that it's all my fault."

"And you'll say what? That we went for a walk in the park and started kissing and lost all sense of time?"

"Well, *something* along those lines."

"To my *dad*?"

"Is he a really fierce old-fashioned kind of *father* dad?" said Russell. "Maybe I won't come *all* the way home with you."

"Don't, then! Look, you go off back to Pembridge Park. It's going to take you ages. I don't even know if there's a bus at this time."

"So I'll take a taxi. No problem. And I was *joking*, Ellie. Of course I'm not going to let you go haring off on your own. I just wish you wouldn't walk so quickly. I can't keep up with you. I'm useless at running."

"So am I!" I have to slow a little because my heart is pounding and I can hardly breathe and sweat is trickling down my back. Oh God, please let my deodorant keep working, please please please. Don't let him think of me as *Smelly* Ellie.

"So you're not a sporty girl. Not jolly hockey sticks?"

"I *hate* hockey. Mags and Nadine and I still do our best to slope off sharpish whenever there's a match." I take a huge gasping breath. "I'm going to have to start running again, Russell. That's quarter past striking. How did it get so *late*?"

"You were in amazing company, that's how," said Russell. "Hey, will your dad be seriously cross, Ellie?"

I don't know! I've never really been out late like

this before. I didn't ever go out on proper dates with Dan—and *no* dad would worry about what I was getting up to with Dan anyway. Dan had total nerd written right through him, like a stick of seaside rock. He used to turn peppermint pink whenever he came up close to me. If he'd ever kissed me like Russell he'd have gone magenta and exploded. Like the girl's head in *Girls Out Late*. And I'm a girl out later than late and Dad and Anna must be seriously worried. They'll worry even more if I tell them the absolute truth. Right, I'll spin them a little story. I'll say I went back to Nadine's and she showed me her favorite horror video, *Girls Out Late,* and it was so compulsive we just couldn't stop watching and lost all track of time. It's not really a lie. I *have* watched part of *Girls Out Late* at Nadine's. They'll understand. They'll be cross, of course. They'll wonder why I didn't phone. OK, OK, I'll say I *tried* to phone but I couldn't get through. No, Nadine's phone was out of order—even her dad's mobile. How about little green aliens landed at Nadine's and they abducted all of us and sabotaged the telephones???

We're nearly at the top of my road now.

"You go, Russell, please."

"But I want to help you out, explain to your dad."

"No, I'm going to tell him I was with Nadine," I say. "Go on, Russell, you go home."

"OK then. Well, after one more kiss. Come on, you're this late, another second isn't going to make much difference."

He takes me in his arms. I'm out of breath to start with—and this last kiss is so amazing I stop breathing altogether. When he eventually lets me come up for air, I'm gasping like a goldfish.

"Oh, Ellie!" says Russell, reaching for me again.

"No! I must go. Bye, Russell—bye!" I wrench myself away and start running again. Running and running and running right down my road to my house. Oh God, what am I going to say? Think, Ellie, think. Take a deep breath. It might be all right. They might have gone to bed early or something. Who am I kidding? The lights are blazing downstairs.

I put my key in the door—and before I can even get it out, Dad wrenches open the door. *He* is blazing.

"Ellie! Where the hell have you been?"

"Oh, Ellie, we've been ever so worried!" Anna pushes past him and gives me a hug. She clings to me as if she's really really glad I'm safe. But then she pushes me away again, almost as angry as Dad. "Why didn't you *phone*? The shops close at *nine*."

"I'm sorry, I'm sorry—it's just we went to McDonald's after, Nadine and Magda and me," I say.

"And?" says Dad.

"And we just got talking, you know what we're like."

"I don't know what you're like anymore, Ellie," says Dad. "I never thought you'd start behaving like this. You've no idea what you put us through."

"I'm *sorry*. Look, I'm really tired now, can we all just go to bed?"

"No we can't. We're going to have this out now."

"Look, maybe we should all go to bed and discuss it in the morning," says Anna.

"For God's sake, you're the one who has been in tears for the last hour!" says Dad.

I stare at Anna. Her eyes are red.

"Why were you *crying*?" I say. "I mean, I can see why you're cross, but there was no need to get *upset*."

"Our thirteen-year-old daughter out God knows where, nearly two hours late home. Come *on*, Ellie!" says Dad. He goes into the kitchen and puts the kettle on. He reaches for the coffee mugs, slamming them hard down on the table—as if he'd like to slam me down hard too.

"Look, I don't know why you're getting so shirty with me, Dad. OK, OK, I'm late home, but it's not that heinous a crime, is it? You're often ever so late home yourself."

"Don't get smart with me, Ellie. Now, tell me, where have you been?"

"You know where I've been, at Flowerfields—and then McDonald's. You're acting like I've been popping pills all night at some rave, for God's sake."

"Where did you go *after* McDonalds?"

"Well, we were there ages."

"Who's we?"

"Dad! Magda, Nadine and me, honestly."

"And then what did you do?"

"Well, Magda went home, and I went back on the bus with Nadine—and I just popped in her house to see some stuff and she started showing me this really creepy video, *Girls Out Late,* and I suppose I stayed a bit late watching it, goodness knows why, because you know I hate horror movies and this one is really truly *gross.*"

Dad and Anna are staring at me. I burble on and on, making stuff up about the movie. The kettle boils. Dad looks as if he should have steam spiraling out of his ears likewise. He makes the drinks, stirring so fiercely coffee slops all over the place.

"So you were at Nadine's?" he says.

"Yes."

"Oh, Ellie," Anna says.

My heart is thumping. This is all going horribly wrong.

"And then where did you go?" Dad says.

"Home."

"By yourself?"

"Well, it's only a few streets."

"You know you're not allowed out after dark by yourself."

"Yes, well, I didn't think it would really matter, just from Nadine's home to here. I suppose I could have rung you."

Oh no! I suddenly remember. I told Anna I *would* ring from Nadine's. I look at her and she shakes her head sadly.

"We waited for you to ring. And then we rang Nadine's—and Nadine's mother said Nadine had come home on her own," Anna says.

I swallow. "What did Nadine say?" I whisper.

"She came out with a whole load of stupid evasions and downright lies," says Dad. "She couldn't seem to see how badly we needed to know where the hell you were."

"So you've been bullying Nadine, too," I say.

"Ellie, nowadays you can't just have a thirteen-year-old out late by herself—not without going out of your mind with worry. Surely you can see that?" says Anna.

"And *eventually* Nadine tells us you've gone off with some boy you picked up in McDonald's," says Dad.

"I didn't pick him up! He talked to me first," I say indignantly.

"A complete stranger! And you went off on your own with him. Are you mad?"

"He's a Halmer's boy," I say.

"Well, they're the worst. They're famous for it. Picking up silly little girls and seeing how far they can go," Dad thunders.

"Don't, you're making all this horrible. Russell isn't a bit like that. He likes *art,* he was sketching and I was sketching, that's how we got talking—and then he came on the bus with Nadine and me and then afterwards we just had this little walk. We were talking about all sorts of stuff, that's all."

"That's all?" says Dad. "You've got your makeup smudged all over your face, Ellie. It's obvious what you've been up to."

"I haven't been up to anything! Stop it! I don't know why you're being like this, spoiling everything."

"Your dad doesn't want to spoil anything, Ellie. He's just been so worried wondering if you were all right. He's overreacting. I am too. It's just this is the first time this has happened and we're obviously getting het up over nothing," says Anna. She takes a sip of coffee, then tries to smile as if this is a normal conversation. "This Russell sounds really nice. Are you going to see him again?"

"Tomorrow."

"No you're not," says Dad.

"Dad! Look, what *is* this? I thought you were really cool about any kind of boyfriend stuff."

"It's not about boyfriends, it's about you lying to us."

"I'm sorry, I just said the first thing that came into my head."

"It's frightening, you seemed so plausible. I just can't believe it of you, Ellie. And I *hate* the idea of you going off on your own with the first boy that beckons in your direction, letting him slobber all over you in the dark."

"Shut up, Dad. Who are you to talk anyway? You've done enough slobbering yourself, as you so charmingly put it. I remember all those girls you went out with after Mum died, before Anna. Maybe *after* Anna too."

"How dare you!" says Dad.

"I do dare. I'm sick of you. Why is there always one rule for adults and another for teenagers? What gives you the right to tell me how to be-have?"

"Stop it, Ellie," Anna says sharply.

"Why should I? And why should I do what *you* say anyway? You're not my mother."

I push past both of them and run upstairs. Eggs is standing in his pajamas on the landing.

"You're in big trouble, Ellie," he whispers.

"You shut up," I say, and go into my bedroom and slam the door.

I flop down on my bed and burst into tears. I hate them all. Why did they have to spoil the most magical evening of my life?

rhyme time

Breakfast is terrible. Dad and I aren't speaking. Anna talks enough for both of us, chitchatting to try and pretend this is a perfectly normal morning. Eggs is intrigued and delighted by all of this, and asks endless idiotic questions about "Ellie's Boyfriend."

"He is *not* my boyfriend. He is just a boy in Year Eleven I happened to meet yesterday and we had a good long chat about art."

"And a good long encounter in the park afterwards," says Dad bitterly, breaking his silence.

"Please!" says Anna, nearly in tears. "Don't talk to Ellie like that."

"I'll talk to her how I damn well please," says Dad, pushing his plate away and standing up. "She's still a child, and she is going to have to learn to do as she's told. She's not staying out till all hours."

"Dad, I was home at twenty past eleven. Heaps of girls in my year stay out till way past midnight."

"I don't care what anyone else does, although

from my conversation with Nadine's parents last night it was all too humiliatingly clear they were obviously appalled. It was evident that Nadine would never behave like that."

This is so infuriating! If only they knew! Last term when Nadine had this thing with this total creep, Liam, she sneaked off and saw him all the time and she lied her little head off to her mum and dad, forever making out she was round at my place or Magda's. But obviously I can't tell Dad this because I don't want to tell tales on Nadine. So I just sigh deeply and tap my fingers on the table, acting like I'm too bored for words.

This winds Dad up so much he starts really yelling at me. Eggs stops thinking it's funny and hunches down in his chair, sucking his thumb. I start to feel scared too. Dad's acting like he really can't stand me. I just don't get it. Why does he have to be so *horrible*? I try to stare him out and act like I'm not even listening but my throat hurts and my eyes have gone all blurry behind my glasses.

"Will you please *stop it*," says Anna, standing up too. "You're frightening Eggs. Dear God, you're frightening all of us. Now *please*—go to school. We'll talk about it tonight, when we've all calmed down."

"I'm out tonight, there's a faculty meeting," says

Dad. "I'll have a sandwich at work and go straight on to the meeting. I'll be back around ten."

I shall be out too, seeing Russell.

Dad's staring at me—and it's as if his mean narrowed eyes can laser through my skull and see what's in my mind.

"*You're* not allowed out, Ellie. You do understand that? You're completely grounded."

"Oh please! What a stupid expression. *Grounded!* It's like something out of prep school."

This is a clever diversionary tactic. It's always the easiest way to score points off Dad. He likes to act like this ultra-lefty alternative guy and yet Grandma and Grandpa are ultra-straitlaced and right-wing and posh and Dad got sent right through the public school system. It's something he's very embarrassed about. He does his best to talk down, but the odd little phrase creeps into his conversation every now and then and betrays him.

"You might find the expression stupid, Ellie— but I trust you understand what it means?"

"I'm not allowed out, right?"

"That's right."

"Not at all?"

"Not at all."

"Oh great, I can't go to school then, can I? So I'll just go back to bed for a nice long snooze."

"Ellie, acting like a six-year-old is not going to

convince me that you're old enough to stay out half the night with strangers," says Dad, and he walks out of the kitchen.

He doesn't say goodbye to me, he doesn't even say goodbye to Anna and Eggs. He just stomps out of the room, still acting like some Victorian control freak dad, like he's Mr. Barrett of Wimpole Street and I'm poetic Elizabeth. Only I'm not reclining on a sofa, I'm on a hard kitchen stool—and I'm not about to elope with my romantic Mr. Browning. Russell and I are hardly at the eloping stage. I don't know whether he writes poetry or not. I don't even know his second name. But I'm going to find out. I'm meeting Russell tonight if it kills me. And Dad very likely *will* kill me if he finds out.

I don't tell Anna my plans. She might well ring Dad up at work and tell on me. She's acting like she's really upset.

"Don't mind your dad too much, Ellie," she says anxiously.

"I won't, don't worry!"

"That's not what I meant! Oh, Ellie, I wish I knew what to say. It's so awful. I can see everyone's point of view. I think your dad overreacted—but you were very very rude."

I open my mouth and she shakes her head.

"Don't say any more, Ellie, please. You've said more than enough."

I feel mean. I know I shouldn't have put in that cheap dig last night about Dad playing around. A while ago, Anna did get ever so worried that he might be having an affair with one of the students at the art college. I suppose it's not surprising she worries because Anna was once at the art college herself. That's when she met my dad. He *is* out an awful lot, though he's always got some excuse, like this meeting tonight. If I were Anna I'd really have it out with him—but she always likes to pretend everything is perfect. She doesn't stand up to Dad the way she should. *I* haven't always stood up to Dad either. But now I've shown him he can't bully me!

"I'm sorry I said some of that stuff last night. I didn't mean to hurt you. It's just *him*," I say. "He can't treat me like that, giving me his orders."

"You are his daughter, Ellie."

"That doesn't give him automatic ownership of me! You might let him walk all over you, Anna, but I'm not going to let him do it to me."

And with that Supergirl swoops out of the kitchen and gathers up her schoolbag.

"You haven't finished your breakfast."

I grab my toast and say I'll eat it on the way to school.

"I'm in a hurry," I say, and dash off.

I'm not in a hurry to go to school. I'm in a hurry

to see Nadine and Magda and tell them everything.

But by the time I make it to school the bell has
already gone and Mrs. Henderson, our form
teacher, is in a right mood this morning. When I
get Magda and Nadine in a corner and start my
story she tells me to stop gossiping and get down
to the gym in double-quick time.

Mrs. Henderson is also the PE teacher, worst
luck. I positively *hate* PE, whether it's hockey or
netball or athletics or rounders. You get hot and
sweaty and people yell at you and you feel stupid.
Well, *I* do. Nadine's pretty hopeless too—and
though Magda can be quite nippy and she's good
at ballwork she generally hangs around with us
and doesn't try, just to be matey.

So the three of us get into a little huddle in the
changing rooms and I start for a second time, but
Mrs. Henderson hounds us again, telling us to cut
the cackle and get changed or we'll be for it.

"Oh, Mrs. Henderson, I'm having a really heavy
period. Can I be excused games today because of
my stomach cramps?" I wail, clutching my tummy.

"Ooh, me too, Mrs. Henderson," says Nadine.
"It's really bad."

"And me too, Mrs. Henderson," says Magda,
determined not to be left out.

Mrs. Henderson puts her hands on her hips.

"So you are all three having your periods?" she says, eyebrows raised.

"It's a very strange but true phenomenon that women living in close circumstances menstruate at exactly the same time," I say. This is a fact. I've read it somewhere, anyway. Even though it doesn't actually apply to Nadine and Magda and me. It would be kind of creepy. And what if you found you needed to do everything else in unison too, so you all woke up at exactly the same time and had to make a dash for the loo simultaneously?

"It's a very strange but true phenomenon that lazy schoolgirls will concoct any silly excuse whatsoever to get out of games," says Mrs. Henderson. "I don't care if you three girls are about to have *babies*—you are still going out on the games field and you will take *exercise*."

We are forced to take so much exercise that I can't even speak the rare times I stagger near Magda or collapse beside Nadine. I just gasp helplessly like a goldfish.

Mrs. Henderson keeps us hop, skip and jump-jump-jumping until the bell goes, which is incredibly mean because we have to charge back to the changing rooms and shower and shove on our clothes in a frantic rush as we only have a five-minute changeover period and it's Mrs. Madley next lesson. A double period—just enough to give everyone stomach cramps! Mrs. Madley takes us for English and it's my second-favorite subject (art first, of course) but Mrs. Madley is megastrict and the one thing she really gets mad about is if we're late for her lesson, which we are.

She rants on as if it's all our fault, and when Magda explains we were still dashing around the athletics field in our PE kit when the bell went, Mrs. Madley says that's no concern of hers, *her* concern is her lesson and we are late, and that is inexcusable. She wastes a good ten minutes telling us we can't afford to be late because we've got so much to do, and when she eventually starts the lesson it's *poetry*. I like a good story, not airy-fairy poems. Especially as she wants us to concentrate on nature poetry. It is not in *my* nature to like nature. It sucks. I should have TOWNIE tattooed on my forehead. We have this awful moldering holiday cottage halfway up a mountain in the wettest part of Wales and every hour I'm forced to spend there seems to last as long as a week.

Mrs. Madley glares at our groans and reads us examples from the Romantic poets. I perk up a little at the word *Romantic* but it doesn't mean *romance*. I don't know what romantic countryside these Romantic poets tramped through but *I* never stand transfixed on my little Welsh hill and admire the fair musk-rose blooms or mellow fruits—

there's just a lot of rank vegetation and mud everywhere.

Then she swaps to modern poetry and she reads a Sylvia Plath poem about blackberrying and I suddenly sit up and listen because I like it, it's so sharp and strange, but then she starts another poem called "Wuthering Heights" and the first line says something about horizons ringing her like faggots and we all collapse and Mrs. Madley gets very narked indeed and says we're all utterly pathetic and then she says *we* all have to write a poem now. Straightaway. At least twelve lines. On Nature. And any girl who fails to do so will get a detention and double English homework.

I struggle.

I think of Wales. I think hard.

Mud, mud, horrible mud.

It's like that old hippopotamus song.

If you slip in the mud
You fall down with a thud.

I think Mrs. Madley requires a more passionate response to Nature.

I try again.

Up in the mountain
Through the glen

You will always wonder when
You can clear off
Home again.

I peer round the room. Help! Everyone else
seems to have got stuck in straightaway. Nadine
rolls her eyes at me and Magda sticks out her
tongue, but their eyes are vague. Concentrating
on their poems. The entire class is looking serious. I daren't do something silly and jokey. But
how can I act like I *care* about the countryside?
Hang on. Nature doesn't stop bang at every town
boundary. I could write about Nature here. I peer
out of the window. It is a gray dreary day. The
privet hedges of the suburban gardens over the
road are cut into ugly arcs. The bedding plants
are crude poster paint colors, set out in unattrac-
tive repeating patterns, like wallpaper. The trees
have all been pollarded so their branches don't
wave in the wind. Suburban nature is not a
pretty sight.

OK. What about in the dark? In the park. Me in
the park with Russell, and the moon above and
the poplar trees? *Yes.*

I write. I forget this is my English lesson and
Mrs. Madley is in a mood and my tights are all
skew-whiff because I pulled them up too quickly
after PE and my hair has gone even wilder than

usual so it's spiraling up and out like there's been a minor explosion in my head.

I'm not here at all. I'm back in the park with Russell, and the key words form on the page, my hand writing as if it's got a will of its own.

"Time's up, girls," says Mrs. Madley. "Right, you've all been very busy. I hope the fruits of your labor are mellow. Who's going to read first?"

Oh no. She wants us to read them out *loud*! I sit, heart thudding. She picks Jess first and Jess reads out this neat little poem about flowers, simple and safe. Then Stacy gets chosen and she gushes on about the sea, the wild white horses and the flying foam until she's practically foaming at the mouth too. It is a totally phoney poem with Absolutely Awful Annoying Alliteration but Mrs. Madley goes a bundle on this too. She picks poor shy Maddie next, who blushes and says hers is rubbish and then she whispers it so we can barely hear. Stuff about mills and fields and harvests and yields. Mrs. Madley doesn't look impressed but says very good, dear. Then she picks Nadine.

"Mine's about night, Mrs. Madley," says Nadine.

It's good, too, very Gothic, a total stormy night with bats flying and cats stalking and trees tapping on windows and flashes of lightning like spears from hell and the crash of thunder as the devil rides out.

"You've really tried hard, Nadine. Well done," says Mrs Madley. "Now . . . *Ellie*."

Oh God. My eyes flash over the page. No, I can't.

"Ellie?"

"Er—mine's about the night too. It's similar to Nadine's. It'll be so repetitive, night after night. Can't we have a day poem instead?"

"Ellie, I'm used to you girls being repetitive. Now start reading."

"Night in the park
The pale moon bare
Luminous above the poplar trees—
Tall thin dark
A giant feather frieze
Surrounding the soft square."

I stop and swallow. I feel my face going red.

"Go on," says Mrs. Madley. "It's good, Ellie."

"That's it," I say. "I've finished."

"No you haven't. I can see there's another verse. And I stipulated a bare minimum of twelve lines. I can count, Ellie."

I take a deep breath.

"Hold me in the park
Your pale face intent
Luminous above mine
Tall, thin, dark
Around me twine
Surrounding, savoring, spent."

There's a gasp and then the entire class explodes. Mrs. Madley stares at me, and then she sighs. Heavily.

"Quieten down, you idiotic girls. Eleanor Allard, what did I ask you to write?"

"A poem, Mrs. Madley."

"What sort of poem?"

"On Nature."

"Did I ask for adolescent soft pornography?"

"No, Mrs. Madley."

"That's right. It seems to me unbelievably stupid to waste your poetic talent and my valuable lesson time on such nonsense. You will do double homework. An essay on nature poetry and another nature poem—and on Monday you will read it out aloud and if anyone so much as titters at the content you will start all over again. Do I make myself plain?"

As plain as a pikestaff. What *is* a pikestaff? Some sort of weapon? *She's* a deadly weapon. A member of staff with the features and ferocious nature of a pike. It's so unfair. I wasn't trying to be insolent—I just got carried away thinking about Russell and me in the park. And it was a poetical comment, contrasting Nature with *human* nature. Mean old bag!

Nadine and Magda are mouthing messages at me but I daren't respond with Mrs. Madley in this mood. What's the matter with all the teachers today? I can't stick school. I go off into a private dream about when I'm grown up and I have my own little studio flat and I can draw all day. Maybe it could be a *big* studio flat with two desks. I could work at one end of the studio, Russell at the other . . .

I am mad, I've only just met him and already I'm thinking about living with him. I wonder what it would be like spending all the day with him. And then all the night too . . .

I jump when the bell goes, startled right out of Russell's arms. Magda and Nadine pounce on me the moment we're outside the classroom.

"Tell us what happened with Russell, Ellie!"

"Your poem! God, you really spelt it out. How could you read it out in front of the entire *class*?"

"I didn't want to. She made me."

"But you wrote it in your English book, you idiot."

"Yes, well, the words just came."

"Like Russell!" says Magda, and she and Nadine hoot with helpless laughter.

"So you actually did it with Russell?"

"I can't believe it when you've only just met him."

"And you lectured me like crazy about not going too far with Liam."

"You were careful, weren't you, Ellie?"

"What was it *like*?"

"Tell us absolutely every little detail."

I stare at them like they've gone bananas.

"OK, OK, he kissed me. Once. Several times."

"And?"

"And that's it."

"But you made it out in your poem you did it."

"No I didn't."

"You did, you did. Here, give us it."

Magda snatches my English book and fumbles for my poem. She reads the last line—and she and Nadine curl up laughing again.

"What?"

"You put *spent*."

"Yeah, I know it sounds a bit odd."

"I'll say."

"But, I wanted an *s* word to make it alliterative, right, seeing as Mrs. Madley's so hot on it—and it had to rhyme with *intent* and it was all I could come up with."

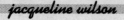

"Can you believe it, Nadine!" says Magda, sighing and raising her eyebrows.

"Oh, *Ellie!* You mean you didn't *mean spent?*"

"I meant—well, we spent time together, the evening was spent—it was the end. What else could I mean?"

"It sounded like you and Russell—you know. So then he was *spent.*"

"Oh my God, I didn't mean *that.* No one thought I meant that, did they?"

"That's what we all thought you meant. Including Mrs. Madley."

"No wonder she's given me all this extra homework."

"So you and Russell didn't really do anything," said Nadine, sounding disappointed. "The way your dad was creating you'd have thought you'd both eloped."

"I'm sorry, I feel awful about him harassing you."

"No problem. I just wish I could have invented some satisfactory excuse for you. I didn't know what to say."

"Neither did I. He's still really mad at me. He says I'm not allowed out at all now."

"What—*ever?*"

"For the foreseeable future. Of course I'm not taking any notice. I'm seeing Russell tonight."

"Really! Wow, he must be keen."

"So are you just going to walk out or what?"

"Well, Dad's not going to be at home so it's sim-ple."

"What about Anna?"

"Oh, she's no problem," I say lightly—hoping it's true.

"You're so lucky, Ellie. My mum's my *big* prob-lem," says Nadine.

"So you're really stuck on Russell?" says Magda.

We're sitting down in the canteen by this time, eating school pizza. Magda's licking up her melted cheese strands. Her little pink cat tongue is very pointed. Her tone is a little pointed too.

"Well . . ." I shrug. I wish I knew what Magda and Nadine think of him. I don't want to act like I'm going overboard if they think he's a total upper-class anorak. On the other hand, if they're dead impressed and envious then I want to act like I'm really enthusiastic, that he's ultra-keen. And he is—isn't he?

What about me? I wish I knew! Sitting here eat-ing pizza in my gungy school uniform I feel almost like I made him up. I'm glad I've got Nadine and Magda as witnesses to the fact that he actually ex-ists.

I can't quite conjure his face up now. I know longish hair. I know brown eyes, but that's about it. I'm not even a hundred percent sure of his voice. Is he really posh or just sort of ordinary? There's one thing I do remember vividly. The feeling of his mouth on mine.

"Ellie! You're blushing."

"I'm not," I protest foolishly, though my face is red hot.

"Are you *sure* you didn't do anything else but kiss?" says Nadine.

"Sure!"

"What's he like at kissing?" asks Magda.

"Good!"

"Mmm—that sounds heartfelt. Better than Dan?"

"I'm sure *Eggs* is a better kisser than Dan."

Dan was never a real boyfriend anyway, whereas Russell . . . Can I call him a boyfriend yet? I know one thing, I simply have to see him tonight—and there's nothing Anna can do about it.

It's hard all the same. Anna has a lovely little snack of fruit bread and soft cheese and plums waiting for me when I get back from school. We have a little munch together while she tells me all about Eggs's new little girlfriend in Year Three—an older woman! Eggs gollops down half a bag of plums and smiles smugly whenever Mandy's name is mentioned.

"It was a bit bold of you to chat her up, seeing as she is in the juniors," I say.

"*She* was the one who chatted *me* up," says Eggs, biting into another plum. "She thinks I'm sweet. She wants me to play with her every day."

"She won't think you're sweet tomorrow when you're stuck in the boys' bogs with terrible diarrhea after eating all those plums," I say.

"It's Saturday tomorrow, so I won't *be* at school, ha ha ha," says Eggs, and he puts an entire whole plum in his mouth.

"Eggs! Don't be so greedy and disgusting. Oh God, you'll choke," says Anna, leaping up and bashing him on the back.

The plum flies out of Eggs's mouth and lands with a messy *phut* on the kitchen floor.

"My plum!" Eggs protests, about to pick it up.

"It's all grimy now," says Anna, whisking it away.

"So is Eggs," I say. "Look at him, he's *filthy*."

"He had finger painting today," says Anna. "Only in Eggs's case it was more like entire-body painting. Shall we give you a bath, little chap?"

"Oh, I want a bath," I say quickly.

Anna looks at me. I usually have my bath late at night. I only have a bath early if I'm going out. She hesitates. We haven't even referred to the tempestuous events of last night and this morning. I can see her struggling, not wanting to spoil our friendly time unless it's absolutely necessary.

I whiz out of the kitchen before she makes up her mind—up to the bathroom, where I wash hurriedly, glad that the hot bath has steamed up the mirror. After my stupid anorexic bulemic blip I'm trying hard to accept my body the way it is—but the way it is is P-L-U-M-P. When you're about to go out on your first serious date you'd *so* much rather look skinny! I pull on my best trousers and a lacy top, decide they look way too tight (why did I have three slices of fruit bread?), put on my baggy trousers and a shirt, decide I look too casual, put on a dress, which looks much too *dressy*, stand in my knickers and search my entire wardrobe, and *eventually* shove my best trousers and lacy top back on.

Time is tick-tocking faster and faster. I do my makeup, doing a serious cover-up job of every weeny snippet of a spot. I outline my eyes to make them look big and beguiling and put mascara on my lashes so I can flutter them provocatively. I leave the lipstick out altogether as I don't want to smear it all over Russell. Then it's hair raking time. I flex my muscles, brandish my fiercest hairbrush, and do my best to tame it—though it's curlier than ever from getting damp in the bath. I still hate the way I look when I've finished, but I looked *worse* yesterday and yet I was the one Russell sketched. Not Magda, not Nadine. Me.

That's still so amazing I can hardly take it in.

"Me me me me me!" I sing, sounding like an opera singer warming up.

Then I go downstairs, steeling myself. I *could* just charge up the hall and out the front door without saying anything. Maybe it would be easier all round?

"Ellie?" Anna calls. She comes to the kitchen door. "You're going out!"

"Bye, Anna," I say, trying to act perfectly normal.

"Ellie! Your dad says you're not allowed out."

"I know, but he's not here."

"Oh for God's sake, don't do this to me! Ellie, you *can't* go out, not after last night."

"You know Dad overreacted."

"Maybe he did a bit, OK—but if you go out now he's never going to back down over this."

"He won't know. I'll be home long before him."

"I should tell him."

"But you won't, will you?"

"*I* don't know. Look, Ellie, can't you invite this Russell round here? That way you could still see him and not defy your dad."

"I don't know his phone number. I don't even know his second name. That's why I have to go and meet him, Anna. If I don't he'll just think I've stood him up and then I'll never see him again."

"And you really like him?"

"Yes! Oh, Anna, please. I've got to go and see him."

"I *can't* just let you go off with him. What if anything happened?"

"What could happen? Look, we're meeting at Flowerfields. I expect we'll go to McDonald's. Or maybe for a pizza, I don't know. I'll explain that I have to get back early—really early. By nine. Well, nine-thirty, say. Please, Anna. Please let me go. I *promise* I'll get back by nine-thirty. I won't let you down. Please trust me. *Please.*"

"Oh go on then, you bad girl," says Anna, and she even gives me another fiver.

I throw my arms round her and give her a big kiss. "You're a darling," I say, and I rush off.

I'm so thrilled she's let me go that I bounce up the road. It isn't until I'm on the bus into town that I start to get nervous. I wonder what I'm going to say when I see Russell. "Hi, Russell," I mutter to myself, grinning and giving little waves. Oh God, someone's staring at me. They'll be wondering about the mad girl sitting muttering and waving to herself. I am starting to get very hot inside my lacy top. It's quite cheap lace so it's itchy. I'm scratching myself with both hands. Now everyone will think I've got *fleas*.

I must keep still when I meet Russell. No more grins, mutters, waves and definitely no more scratching—otherwise he'll sketch me as a monkey.

The bus is taking forever. I'm scared I'm going to be late, and he'll think I'm not coming. Oh, Russell, of *course* I'm coming. I've braved my dad, I've bullied poor Anna—I've chanced everything to see you.

I leap off the bus as soon as it gets into town. I run wildly all the way to Flowerfields Shopping Centre. I pull up, panting, with one minute to spare. I'm *first*.

And last. This is why.

I wait.

Russell is late.

I wait and wait and wait.

Russell is very very very late.

I wait until eight.

And then I trail home, trying not to cry.

doom and gloom time

"Oh, Ellie, thank goodness. You are a good girl! But you didn't have to come back this early," says Anna.

Then she sees my face.

"Ellie? Oh dear. What happened? Wasn't he so nice this time? Did he do anything to upset you?"

"He didn't do anything. He didn't turn up!" I wail, and then all the tears inside me gush like the waters in *Titanic*.

Eggs is in bed, thank God, and Dad is out of course. So it's just Anna and me. She puts her arms round me and I howl on her shoulder. She's wearing a new pale blue sweater her friend Sara gave her and I'm wearing a lot of mascara.

"Oh God, Anna, I've got black splodges all over your sweater. I'm so sorry," I burble.

"Never mind. I don't actually like this sweater anyway—simply because Sara shows off so much about designing her own-label clothes. She thinks I'm dotty about her stuff but I only bought it to be polite."

"I'll have it off you if you don't like it."

"I wonder why you want to wear everyone *else's* sweaters," says Anna, mopping at my face with a tissue.

"I draw the line at Dad's," I say. "Oh, Anna, don't tell him Russell didn't turn up, will you?"

"Of course not. I'm not even telling him you went out! I'm so sorry, Ellie—but I'm so relieved you're OK. I *shouldn't* have let you go out. Not because of your dad. It's really not safe for a girl your age to go out by herself."

"Yes it is. All too safe. No one wants to have their wicked way with me. Certainly not Russell. Oh, Anna, it was so awful waiting there. All these girls were hanging around and they kept looking at me and giggling. It was totally obvious they knew I'd been stood up."

"You're sure it was tonight you were supposed to be meeting?"

"Yes, the time, the place, everything. He obviously didn't mean it. Dad was *right*. He wasn't the slightest bit interested in me. He just wanted to try it on."

"Did he?" Anna asked, alarmed.

"No. We just kissed."

I think about Russell's kisses—and how special they were to me and yet he obviously doesn't want to kiss me ever again. I cover my face and sob.

"Poor old Ellie. Don't take it to heart. I've been

stood up before. So has everyone. Don't get so upset. Look, why not phone Nadine or Magda? Have
a good moan to them."

But for just about the first time in my life
I can't face talking to my two best friends. I know
they'd be sweet to me, but it would be just so
humiliating, especially after showing off about
Russell so at school and writing that stupid
poem. . . .

I can understand why Nadine would barely talk
to me when she was so cut up about Liam. He was
a hateful pig who just wanted to have sex with
her—but at least he went out with her lots of
times and made her think she was really special.
Russell couldn't be bothered to go out with me
once.

I go upstairs to bed very early, wanting to be
well out of the way before Dad comes home. In
my bedroom, I take out my sketchbook. I look
at the portrait of Russell. Then I take my fattest
blackest crayon and scribble all over it, again and
again until it's just a black crumpled mess. Then I
pull it out of the book and tear it into tiny little
shreds and empty them out of my window. They
flutter into the night air like black confetti.

Right, I've torn him up. Now I shall forget all
about him. He's not worth another thought.

I know this. But I do think about him. Half the

night. I have a lie-in until really late in the morning, huddling right down under the covers so I can't see the daylight. I dimly hear the telephone ringing. Then Anna's light footsteps.

"Phone for you, Ellie."

For one lunatic second I wonder if it could possibly be Russell ringing to apologize—and then I remember he doesn't know my number, he doesn't even know my full name.

It's Magda.

"Were you still in *bed?* So you had a seriously late night with the divine Russell, right?"

"Wrong," I mumble.

"What? Oh, is your dad around?" says Magda.

Dad's actually out at the swimming baths with Eggs. Thank goodness.

I mumble something even less intelligible to Magda.

"I can't *hear* you! Look, just answer yes or no if your dad's earwigging. Did you have a good time with Russell?"

"No."

"Oh, so you had a *bad* time with Russell?"

"No."

"Well, make up your mind!"

"Look, I can't talk about it, Mags."

"Well, meet me this afternoon, OK? And Nadine?"

"I'm not allowed *out*. Dad won't let me," I say, and I put the phone down.

"Your dad *will* let you go out with Magda and Nadine," says Anna.

"I don't feel like it anyway," I say, and I droop back up the stairs.

"Are you going to have a bath?" Anna asks.

I don't feel like having a bath. I don't feel like getting dressed. I don't feel like having breakfast. I don't feel like having any communication with the outside world ever again. I don't even want to talk to Anna anymore.

I go back to my rumpled bed and huddle up, my knees under my chin. I wish I still had my old blue special elephant. I wish I was a really little girl again. I wish I still thought boys were stupid mucky creatures who picked their noses and ate it and yanked the arms off Barbie dolls. I wish Eggs didn't exist and Dad hadn't met Anna. I wish my mum was still alive.

My throat aches and my eyes burn and I start crying because I suddenly miss Mum so much even though she died long ago. I cry under the covers for ages. When I eventually crawl out at lunchtime my eyes are sore and swollen. I come downstairs to have bacon sandwiches. Anna has obviously said something to Dad and Eggs. They both stare at me but after one fierce glance from

Anna they start nattering on about swimming. Eggs demonstrates his version of freestyle so wildly that his sandwich crusts go flying and he nearly pokes me in the eye. Dad tells him to calm down. Eggs gets wilder. Dad gets cross. Anna intervenes. I let it all wash over me. As if I care about any of this stuff. As if I care about anything anymore. It's not like I'll ever have a family of my own. It's obvious no boy is ever going to want to go out with me, let alone form a proper partnership. My first boyfriend, Dan, was a total nerd. Anorak Boy with a capital *A,* and yet even he fell out of love with me. And Russell couldn't even be bothered to turn up on our very first date. I am going to lead a totally solitary unloved uncherished life.

A tear drips down my cheek.

"Oh, Ellie," says Dad. "I can't bear to see you so miserable. Look, I'm *sorry* I wouldn't let you meet up with this boy yesterday."

I glance at Anna. She raises her eyebrows a fraction. I decide it's safer to say nothing.

"Ellie's crying," says Eggs, unnecessarily.

"Just finish your sandwich, Eggs, and leave Ellie alone," says Anna.

"I feel like I've overplayed the heavy father role," says Dad. "You do understand, Ellie, it was just because I care about you."

No one else cares about me. No need to worry about Russell going too far with me, Dad. Russell doesn't want to get anywhere *near* me.

I don't say any of this. I simply sniff.

"Anna says you told Magda I wouldn't let you meet up with her this afternoon. Ellie, I'm not that mean. You can go out with your girlfriends, for goodness' sake."

I just shrug and shrink back into my bedroom.

But Magda and Nadine don't give up on me that easily. There's a knock at the door ten minutes later. Magda. And Nadine. Dad answers the door and walks right into it.

"Oh, Mr. Allard! Look, we've come round to plead with you," I hear Magda say.

"We know you're cross with Ellie. I'm sorry I didn't tell you what was going on straightaway. It's partly my fault," says Nadine.

They badger and flirt and flutter. Dad is clearly enjoying the situation and lets them carry on for ages. Then he pretends to weaken.

"Well, girls, I'd hate to spoil your afternoon. OK, you've persuaded me. Ellie can go out with you."

They squeal gratefully, then come bounding upstairs. Magda clatter-clatters in her platforms, Nadine bounce-bounces in her trainers. They barge into my bedroom like two knights in armor rescuing a princess. I feel more like the loathsome monster.

They show off about their supposed victory and I try to act grateful.

"Though actually I don't really feel like going out," I protest weakly.

I pretend it's because I've got a bad period. They are as suspicious as Mrs. Henderson. They are both peering at my sore eyes and blotchy face.

"Come *on,* Ellie," says Magda. "Tell us about Russell. Oh God, didn't he turn up?"

"You've got it," I say, and I start sniffing again.

"Oh, Ellie, what a creepy mean rotten thing to do. How long did you wait for him?" says Nadine.

"An *hour*!" I wail.

I tell them all about it. Magda puts her arm round my neck and Nadine puts her arm round my waist and they both pat me sympathetically. Nadine says she thought his eyes were too close together and he had this really seriously shifty look which should have been a warning. But then, she's not one to talk, looking at her and Liam. Magda says he seemed awfully juvenile for his age anyway, just wanting to show off about himself, but she's no one to talk either, she went out with Greg, who had all the sophistication of Dennis the Menace.

I start to feel a bit better. Nadine goes to the

bathroom, comes back with my flannel and bathes
my eyes. Magda whips out her own makeup bag
and powders them deep gray and outlines them in
black and I now have new eyes and old friends
and I feel a *lot* better.

"Coming out now?" says Magda.

Nadine gets my jacket, and off we go, the three
of us. I start to wonder why on earth I was so upset over Russell. Boyfriends are OK, but they aren't
a patch on girlfriends who've stuck by you and
care about you forever.

We go down the town to Flowerfields and I actually manage to be funny about a sad little ghost
of Ellie still standing waiting there. We wander
round the clothes shops for a while, trying on different stuff and hooting with laughter.

"There! I knew you'd cheer up if we took you
out," says Magda. "Forget Russell, forget all boys.
They're not worth it."

At that precise moment her eyes are following
three boys in tight jeans fooling around outside
the HMV shop. They disappear inside.

"I'm wondering about buying that new *Best
Ever Love Songs* compilation album," says Magda.
"Can I go and have another listen?"

Nadine catches my eye and we have a giggle.

We saunter into HMV and Magda eyes up the
boys while Nadine and I have another flip through

our current favorites, playing the If-I-had-a-hundred-quid-to-spend game. The Claudie Coleman album is high on both our lists.

"Hey, look!" says Nadine, pointing to a Claudie Coleman poster above the counter. "She's singing at the Albert Hall next month."

"Oh wow, let's go!" says Magda, actually distracted from the boys. "I'd love to see her in person, wouldn't you?"

"Well, the tickets would be seriously pricey," I say cautiously, wishing I wasn't always so strapped over cash. "But maybe Anna would help me out."

"Look, I'll help you out if needs be—and you too, Nadine," says Magda. "But us three girls have simply *got* to go and see Claudie, right?" She's scribbling down the phone number for the ticket office. "I'll get my dad to book them on his credit card the minute I get home, OK?"

We take it in turns singing along with Claudie at the listening station. There's one particular tune that I can't get enough of. Claudie's singing very close up, soft and breathy, like she's whispering in your ear.

"Don't even think about him
He's not worth it, worth it, worth it.
Who needs a man to feel a woman?
You're doing fine without him, girl."

I replay it till I know it off by heart and we sing it as we go all around Flowerfields. I sing it as a duet on the bus with Nadine. She's bought the album, lucky thing, but she's promised to do a tape for me. Then I hum a solo version as I walk back from her house.

Who needs Russell? Who cares about Russell? *Don't even think about him.*

"Ellie, guess who came calling round here this afternoon?"

I stand staring and wait.

"Guess," says Dad.

"*I* don't know," I say, shrugging.

"A certain young man."

I miss a beat.

"*Which* young man?"

"With floppy hair. Rather full of himself. Sketchbook tucked slightly pretentiously under his arm."

"Russell!"

"The very one."

"But how did he know where I *live*?"

"Ah. That was my question too. And he had a rather impressive answer. He knew vaguely the area, so he'd worked his way up and down several roads describing a certain young lady called Ellie—and eventually someone somewhere recognized the description and suggested he call at our house."

"Oh my God! Are you *serious,* Dad? Russell really did come round?"

"He did indeed. He was very worried about last night. Russell's dad kicked up merry hell because the lad was late back on Thursday night. Apparently he hadn't deigned to tell his dad he was going walkabout after school and when he sauntered home at midnight he was so angry with him he wouldn't let him out at all yesterday, even though young Russell begged and pleaded and moaned and groaned. So he couldn't meet you at your special trysting place—which is just as well because you were similarly shut up by your equally outraged parent. Yes?"

"Yes, yes, right! So what else did Russell say?"

"Not a lot. He seemed a little dismayed by my reaction. I was extremely angry with the young man. He had no right to purloin you and whisk you off to the park."

"You didn't really get cross with him, did you, Dad? I can't *believe* this. He didn't stand me up? He really couldn't help it? And he went all over the place trying to track me down this afternoon just to explain?"

"*Just* to explain?" says Dad. "He needed to explain until he was blue in the face. Positively ultramarine."

"Oh, Dad, you weren't really heavy with him, were you?"

"You bet I was. That young man won't dare so much as blink in your direction without my say-so. And I say *no*."

I stare at Dad, desperate to suss whether he's serious or not. I think he's teasing me, but I can't be sure. I just wish Anna was here and she could sort him out for me. Why did Russell have to come round when I was *out*, for heaven's sake! But imagine—going from house to house asking for me. That sounds like he's really serious about seeing me!

"So what exactly did he say, Dad?"

"I told you, I did nearly all the talking."

"And how was it left?"

Dad shrugs. "I think he sees the error of his ways."

"*Dad*. I wish you wouldn't be so annoying. I mean, did Russell say anything about . . . seeing me again?"

Dad shakes his head. "Certainly not, seeing as I'd expressly forbidden it."

"You didn't! Really, truly, you said I couldn't go out with him?" I'm still pretty sure he's winding me up but I can hear my voice getting shrill all the same.

"Really, truly . . . possibly!" Dad says.

"Did he suggest seeing me or not?"

"You always insist you're a liberated young woman. Maybe *you* should make the running. *If* I were to allow you out again, which I doubt."

"So how can I make the running, Dad? Did Russell tell you his address?"

"Nope."

"He really didn't?"

Dad shakes his head but he's still got that irritating grin on his face.

"So how can I get in touch with him? Do I have to go on an equivalent quest all around Pembridge Park?"

"You could," says Dad. "Or he could have jotted it down in this letter." He brings out an envelope from his pocket and waves it in the air at me.

I snatch it and tear it open. My eyes skitter down the page. "See you—I *HOPE*! Russell." And a little picture.

My heart is thudding.

"Well?" says Dad.

Aha! It's his turn to be curious.

"Yes, he's very well," I say, smiling.

"And you are now too, I take it?" says Dad.

"Yep." I dance off to the kitchen and make myself a cup of coffee, reading Russell's letter while the kettle boils. Then I read his letter again while I drink my coffee. And again and again.

Dear Ellie,

I'm so so so so extra sorry. I felt so bad about not being able to make it on Friday night. And kind of humiliated too, because my dad went completely off his head and wouldn't let me out simply because he got fussed last night.

I can't believe his attitude—and it's bloody hypocritical too, going on about what I'm getting up to when he's smooching all over our house with his girlfriend. But anyway, he can't keep me locked up permanently. Will you meet me after school on Monday—at McDonald's? I'll be there as soon as I can make it—around twenty to four. I'll wait for you and hope very much that you'll come. I'll be the one looking stupid and saying sorry over and over again.

See you—I HOPE! Russell

He's done a small sketch of himself—floppy hair, earnest expression, pencil in one hand, sketchbook in the other. There are little initial letters on the sketchbook, so tiny I have to hold them up to my eyes and squint. *R L E. Rule? Role?* No, *Russell. R* for *Russell, E* for *Ellie? L? L? L? L? L? L? L? L? L?*

Russell Loves Ellie.

I feel as if I'm on a giant switchback, swooping up and over, up and over, up and over.

"Aren't you making your old dad a cup of coffee too?" says Dad, coming into the kitchen.

"Sure." I shove the letter quickly into my pocket.

"Nice letter?"

"Hmm."

"He wants to see you again?"

"Sort of, yeah."

"So what are you going to do? Your dad expressly forbids it."

"What?" I stare at Dad. "Are you serious?"

Dad is trying to frown but his eyes are twinkling. "Sort of," he says. "Look, Ellie, I got seriously panicky about Thursday night. It's the first time you've ever been out after dark like that and I couldn't stand it."

"I bet you went out with girls when you were my age."

"Maybe that's why I panicked. I remember all too clearly what I was like when I was Russell's age. It makes me cringe now. I didn't treat girls like people. I was trapped in this awful stuffy boys' school so I never knew girls properly. They were just amazing exotic creatures and we were struck dumb in their company and it was like this sick competition seeing how far you could go with them—"

"Dad!"

"I know, I know. And then we'd boast about it afterwards to our mates—exaggerating obviously, saying all this degrading stuff."

"Look, Dad, that was way back when boys were like Neanderthals. Russell isn't a bit like that," I insist, though I feel myself getting pink in the face, remembering the way we kissed.

"I know, I know," says Dad. "As soon as I met him I could see he's just a nice decent kid who wants to be friends with my daughter. He told me you had this long intense conversation about art. He showed me his sketch of you, by the way, and it's *good*. His style needs a bit of fine-tuning but for his age he's got a great sense of line. Anyway, I felt like a total prat. I believed he was a sex-crazed loony slobbering all over you when all the time you were having this totally platonic artistic discussion."

"Yeah, that's just the way it was, Dad, I told you," I say, still pink in the face. "So, as you realize times have changed, is it OK if I go out with Russell? To do some sketching together!"

"That's the thing, Ellie. Times *have* changed. When I was young I stayed out till really late as a teenager and no one turned a hair. Even when

Anna was young she went out to local discos and youth clubs when she was thirteen or fourteen. But now there aren't any harmless little discos, it's all wild raves. And you know I don't want you going anywhere near Seventh Heaven again after they did that drug raid there."

"OK, OK, I promise we won't *go* to Seventh Heaven."

"I don't feel happy about you and Russell going anywhere, Ellie, not after dark. The town is attracting a whole load of yobs who just want to roam around picking fights and getting into trouble. I'm not surprised Russell's dad was really worried about him being out late."

"Russell can look after himself, Dad. He's not some sad little wimp."

"He could be Mr. Muscles Macho Man. It wouldn't make any difference if a whole gang started in on him."

"You're getting totally *paranoid*, Dad."

"Maybe. I don't know. But how about if you and Russell met up after school and then he went back home around nine?"

"Dad! We're not *Eggs's* age!"

"I know, I know—but you're as precious to me as Eggs and I don't need another night like Thursday. Look, you're still supposed to be in the doghouse for that. I'll let you see Russell, but I'm going to stick to this nine o'clock curfew for the time being. I think that's more than fair."

"I don't!"

"Well, it gets dark by nine—so you couldn't do any sketching then, could you?" says Dad, smiling.

I smile back weakly. I don't know who's bluffing who. But at least I can see Russell—even if it's only in daylight!

I go up to my bedroom and read his letter again. Several times more. Then I go downstairs and ring Nadine and tell her that it's all OK and that Russell walked round and round the town looking for me, practically knocking at every house door.

Nadine isn't quite as impressed as I'd hoped. She's got her Claudie album playing full blast (her family are obviously out) and she's singing along instead of concentrating fully. I need to ask her something.

"Nadine, do you really think Russell looks seriously shifty?"

Nadine herself sounds as if she's doing some serious shifting on the other end of the phone. "No, no, Ellie, not at all. I was just, you know, saying stuff to comfort you. I don't think his eyes are too close together either. I think it was just his intense expression when he was sketching you."

I let it go at that. I ring Magda next. She's got some great news for me first—her dad has booked three tickets for us to go and hear Claudie next month! "There, aren't you pleased, Ellie? Claudie will cheer you up. He's not worth it, worth it, worth it, right?"

"Well, maybe he *is* worth it after all, Magda."

I fill her in on all the details, massaging the facts even more impressively, so that I have Russell practically trekking round the entire country looking for me.

I wait for Magda's comments. There's a little silence on the end of the phone.

"So it shows he didn't just stand me up," I say.

"Sorry, Ellie, I'm not quite clear. You mean he stood you up because his dad wouldn't let him go out?"

"He didn't stand me up, he wanted to come."

"But Daddy wouldn't let him."

I don't like that Daddy bit. I pause. "I take it you still think Russell is awfully juvenile, just wanting to show off about himself?"

I can hear Magda swallowing.

"No, no, well, not Russell in particular. Just most boys in Year Eleven. I mean, they're better than the pathetic creeps in Year Ten, not to mention Year Nine, but they're still not exactly . . . mature."

"So you think that Russell is *imm*ature?"

"Oh, Ellie, stop being so prickly. I think all boys are immature, full stop. But your Russell is great . . . for a boy."

I agree happily and tell her to thank her dad for ordering the tickets. Sometime I am going to have to tackle *my* dad about coughing up the cash, but maybe it might be better to wait till tomorrow seeing as we have already spent so long negotiating today.

I decide to put myself in a good light by making him another coffee, even though it's nearly teatime. I wonder where Anna and Eggs have got to. I have to make sure I get Anna on her own to get her to promise to keep quiet about my sneaking out to meet Russell on Friday night. If Dad knows I deliberately disobeyed him then maybe he'll stop me seeing Russell altogether. And I *have* to see him!

I think about him going round all those houses asking for me. It's like a fairy tale. He's the handsome prince on the loopy quest: knock three times on every house in this street and the next and *then* you will find the princess and get to kiss her. . . .

I go into a happy little daze in my bedroom and don't resurface until I hear the front door.

"Is that you, Anna?" I shout.

"No, it's just me," Dad calls. "I was looking

down the road to see if there was any sign of them. I don't know where they've got to."

"Where were they going? Shopping?" I peer over the banisters at him.

"Ellie! As if Anna would go shopping with Eggs. You know what a pain he can be. No, Nadine's mum phoned her up." Dad pulls a face.

I giggle. Nadine's mum is one of those women who seem to spring from their bed fully made up, hair lacquered into a helmet, armed with a J-Cloth and a DustBuster.

"Don't you dare laugh! She's still very much looking down her pointy nose at me because you were out so late on Thursday, and she doesn't want you to be a bad influence on her Nadine."

"Oh God, she wasn't going on about it *again,* was she?"

"For a while, yes. But she was also telling Anna about this local photo shoot she's dragging that showy little sister of Nadine's to this afternoon— and she wondered if Anna wanted to take Eggs."

"What? *Eggs!*"

"I know, I know, I can't really see the little guy prancing around in front of a photographer myself, but apparently this particular company wanted to find little boys who *look* like little boys—that is, filthy dirty and fooling about. It's for this washing powder where a little girl is all dressed up in a pristine party frock—"

"Natasha!"

"And all these little boys come along and get her to play football with them and then push her over and get her all muddy."

"Ah, Eggs might be good at that!"

"That's what Anna thought. He seemed to relish the idea too. And you get paid! So that's where they went. Only they've been gone hours and hours."

"Eggs probably got too enthusiastic and completely coated Natasha in mud. They might have to hose her down and dry her off and pretty her up again for each take—that would take ages."

"And meanwhile we've got rumbly tummies. I suppose I ought to mosey out into the kitchen and get something started for supper."

Dad sounds totally lacking in enthusiasm. He understands the concept of the New Man but has all the laziness and lack of inclination of a very *old* man.

"I'll rustle something up, Dad," I say cheerily, determined to keep in his good books so that he might just extend this ludicrous nine o'clock curfew.

I rustle—and hustle and bustle—and we sit down to burnt omelettes and soggy chips.

"This is delicious," Dad says determinedly. "But the thing is, Ellie, I'm starting to get really worried about Anna and Eggs, so I've sort of lost my appetite."

It's only partly an excuse. He does look a bit tense and twitchy.

"They'll be all right, Dad. This shoot thing will have just gone on for ages. Look, I'll phone Nadine again and ask her how long these things take."

I phone Nadine, but this time Nadine's mum answers. She doesn't sound too thrilled when she hears my voice.

"Oh, it's *you*, Ellie. I hope you've done your best to show you're sorry for your behavior last Thursday night. Your poor parents were in a terrible state. And I wasn't at all happy about you involving my Nadine in your little deception."

She rants on in similar vein for ages. I hold the receiver away from my ear, sighing. Eventually there seems to be a little pause.

"I'm really sorry, but anyway, I just wanted to ask—"

"No, you can't talk to Nadine just now, she's having her supper. You girls! You're on the phone every two minutes and yet you see each other every day. What? No, Nadine—go back to the table! What's that, Natasha, pet?"

"Have you and Natasha just got back from the photo shoot?" I gabble quickly.

"No! No, we've been back since five o'clock. It was a reasonably quick shoot—*no* thanks to your little brother, who ran wild and wouldn't behave sensibly at all. So much so, they didn't even *use* him in the end."

"So where are Eggs and Anna now?" I ask.

"*I* don't know."

"But didn't they come back with you?"

"No. I offered them a lift in my car but Anna had got talking to some strange man and they went off with him."

"Anna went off with a strange *man*?" I say.

Dad comes rushing to the phone. He grabs it from me and starts asking Nadine's mum all sorts of questions.

"I keep telling you, Mr. Allard, I don't know who this man is, or anything about him. I was busy looking after my Natasha. I don't know if he was another parent—although he didn't seem to have a child with him. He wasn't on the main photographic team because I've got to know everyone involved. I suppose he could have been representing the washing powder company—but he didn't look the type. He was wearing a black leather jacket. He seemed a bit rough, like a biker. I was a little surprised to see your wife going off with him."

"So why didn't you try to stop her?" Dad shouts.

"Well, really! *I'm* not responsible for your wife's behavior. Nor your daughter's behavior either. I'd be grateful if you'd stop phoning me up and acting as if it's my fault if one or the other goes missing."

She puts the phone down on us. Dad and I stare at each other.

"Don't look so worried, Dad. Don't take any notice of her, you know what she's like."

"But she's not a liar. She said she saw Anna go off with this strange man. Eggs, too. Dear God, Ellie, what's happened to them?"

"Maybe Nadine's mum made a mistake," I say, though Nadine's mum is like one of those meerkats, all beady eyes and extended neck, seeing absolutely everything. She isn't the sort of woman who ever makes mistakes. But then Anna isn't the sort of woman to disappear with a strange biker, either.

"Anna wouldn't ever go off with a weirdo stranger—especially not with Eggs," I say.

"I know," Dad says wretchedly. "That's what makes it worse. Oh, Ellie, maybe she knows this man."

"What?"

"Maybe—maybe he's a friend of hers. More than a friend."

"Oh, *Dad*."

"Well, I suppose I'm not the easiest man in the world to live with. And—and sometimes I enjoy a little harmless flirt with some of the students. It's nothing serious, I swear, but perhaps it preys on Anna's mind. Then on Thursday night you turned on me and practically accused me of having a girl-friend on the side."

"Dad, I was just trying to *get* to you."

"I know, and it worked, too. And I *haven't* got a girlfriend. I maybe mightn't have always been squeaky clean in the past but I hope I've grown up a bit now. I know I've got a really wonderful wife—"

"You've had two," I say, suddenly fierce.

"Yes, I'm sorry, Ellie. No one can ever replace your mum. We know that. It's been hard for Anna. I don't really treasure her enough. I forget how young she is. She used to be so different when I first met her—"

"Dad, don't."

"You don't think this guy in the leathers is some boyfriend of hers? Someone she met at her Italian class, maybe?"

"Of course not," I say firmly, but Dad's in such

a state he's almost got me wondering. There's a part of me that knows perfectly well that this is totally crazy and my kind, sensible stepmother isn't going to hit the road on a Harley with a secret lover—certainly not with Eggs along too—but then it seems so unlike Anna to be so late and not even phone.

Maybe this strange man was just giving her a lift—but then they had an accident. A crash.

I let myself think just for a second what it would be like if Anna never ever came back. And it's so weird. For years I didn't like her. I felt she *was* taking my mum's place and I just wanted her to get out so it could be Dad and me, even though we were half a family without Mum. But now—Anna's part of this new family. She can be an old ratbag sometimes when she has a nag about homework or the state of my bedroom, but most of the time she's like a special big sister to me.

And what about my real little brother. Heavens, would I actually miss *Eggs*???

"Oh, Dad, they've got to be all right," I say, and he puts his arms round me and holds me tight.

"Of course they are, take no notice of that stupid stuff I said. I'm just ranting rubbish. Of course they're all right. There's obviously some perfectly ordinary explanation. They'll be here any minute now, you wait and see."

And then suddenly there's a key in the door and Eggs calling and they *are* here and the waiting is over.

"Hi! Did you wonder what had happened to us?" Anna says cheerily, while Dad swoops Eggs up in his arms and gives him a huge bear hug.

I feel so relieved that they're safe, so ridiculous for getting worried, so angry that Anna's got me all churned up like this.

"Where have you been? You could have *phoned*!" I say furiously.

Anna stares—then she bursts out laughing.

"What's so funny?" I growl.

"Talk about role reversal! You sound just like a mum," Anna laughs. She looks at Dad, expecting him to join in the laughter.

"We were really worried, Anna," says Dad, releasing Eggs and putting him down on the carpet. "Why didn't you phone? What were you playing at?"

"I'm sorry. I didn't realize you'd be so worried," says Anna, going into the kitchen. "Have you two had your tea? Oh dear, who burnt the frying pan? Hey ho. Eggs, what would you like? Boiled eggs or scrambled?"

"Scrambled me, please," says Eggs, shrieking with laughter, as if this is the most original joke in the entire world, though he's told it every time he's eaten an egg for the past couple of years.

He seems even more full of himself than usual, puffing out his chest and beating it like a little gorilla.

"I'm going to be famous, Ellie," he says.

"I thought you were pretty useless at the photo shoot, not doing what you were told and being silly to Natasha. They didn't even use you," I snub him.

"How did you know?" says Anna, startled.

"Because I phoned Nadine's mum," I explain.

"Oh dear! Yes, she wasn't best pleased with us. She felt we were mucking up Natasha's big moment. I must admit, though, when I saw that child prancing and pouting in front of the cameras I was awfully glad I had an ordinary mischievous little kid like Eggs," says Anna, whisking eggs. "Anyone else want any eggs? Apart from Humpty Dumpty here."

"Do an eggy Humpty jumper, Mum!" says Eggs.

"Hey, yes, that would look *great*. Maybe Humpty could be sitting on the wall on the front and falling off and in pieces on the back," Anna says, giving Eggs a kiss on the nose.

"And it's my woolly jumper, isn't it, Mum? They're all my jumpers and Ellie can't ever ever borrow them, can she?"

"As if I'd want to!" I say witheringly.

"Well, I know you've always thought my funny

jumpers are awful, Ellie—but they might just prove popular," says Anna, stirring eggs. She catches sight of Dad, who is still staring at her. "What?"

"What the hell do you mean, 'What?'" Dad explodes. "I just can't believe this. You disappear with our son for almost the whole day. You're hours and hours late home, you were seen by that dreadful woman going off with this weirdo biker—"

"Biker?" says Anna, looking mystified.

"A man in a black leather biker jacket."

"Oh!" says Anna, giggling.

"It's not funny!" Dad thunders. "For God's sake tell me what you've been up to."

"OK, OK. But a *biker*!" Anna splutters again. "That was George, and the biker jacket is actually an Armani masterpiece that's only seen the inside of his new silver Audi."

"So who the hell is George?" says Dad—and now he sounds *really* worried.

"George is the editor of a new family magazine. Not the tea-cozy and telly type, this is ultra-hip and designer-orientated, right?"

Anna sounds like she's talking a new language. She almost looks like a new person. Her face is glowing, her eyes are big, her hair is a little ruffled in a chic sort of way, her whole stance is different, chin up, chest out, confident. It's as if this George is a fairy godfather and changed her into Cinderella at the ball.

Then she remembers the eggs, rescues them and serves Eggs his tea.

"So what about this George?" I say. "Oh, Anna, has he offered you a job on his magazine?"

"Yes! Well, on a freelance basis, so there's no problem about being here for Eggs," says Anna, dipping toast into Eggs's eggs and nibbling.

"But you don't know the first thing about journalism," says Dad.

"I know. He's offered me a job as a designer," says Anna. She looks at me triumphantly. "It's my jumpers, Ellie! He saw Eggs and asked me where I'd bought his sweater. I said I made it myself so he asked about a pattern and I explained that I sketch the picture out in crosses first and then I knit it up hoping for the best and he was really interested. Then after the shoot (and dear God it was Eggs who needed shooting, he was *so* naughty), George asked if we could go to the magazine offices to talk things over."

"And you did? On a Saturday? Surely it would be all locked up?"

"Darling, George is the *editor*. He can go into his own office whenever he chooses," Anna says.

"You were still a bit reckless agreeing so easily.

He could have been spinning you a line," says Dad.

Anna shakes her head at him. "It's not like he invited me back to his *house*. It was a beautiful state-of-the-art office in Bloomsbury."

"You went all the way to London with him?"

"Yes, I rode in his car and he had his own PlayStation and he let *me* play with it and I got to the third level," says Eggs, his mouth all yellow froth.

"Don't talk with your mouth full, Eggs. Do you want some yogurt now? *Anyway*, George and I talked things through at length—"

"While *we* were sitting here at home wondering what the hell had happened to you. Why didn't you phone?" Dad demands.

"Because I didn't think it would look particularly professional if I said 'Excuse me, I have to phone my husband to stop him worrying about me,'" says Anna. She folds her arms and faces Dad. "I'm sorry you and Ellie got worried but I feel I behaved perfectly responsibly. I don't see why you have to give me the third degree now. I thought you'd be thrilled for me. It's the chance I've been waiting for. I was so envious when Sara started designing her clothes. I felt I'd wasted all my art school training. You've no idea what it's been like never having a job."

"I thought you were happy looking after me and Ellie and Eggs," says Dad.

"I *am* happy—but I don't see why I can't have a career as well, especially now Eggs has begun school."

"And now George really wants Anna-jumpers?" I say.

"He got me to sketch some of the ones I've made already. Of course some of the characters have their own trademark so we can't use them—but I roughed out some new animal ones for him, pigs and piglets in little stripy shirts, a funny cow milkman driving an orange milk cart, a granny sheep knitting a jumper, a chicken painting a Fabergé-type egg. He wants all those designs properly drawn out with the knitting instructions and the jumpers knitted up, of course. He says I can use a professional knitter or two if I don't have time myself, as it's obviously the designs that are important. Then we talked about sweaters in football colors and a set of weather jumpers, a light silky cotton jersey with a sun, a thick double-knit sweater with a snowman, a rainbow-striped sweater with the sun on one side and raindrops on the other. It was weird, once I got started I couldn't stop, all these ideas came tumbling out—and you'll never guess, he's paying me five hundred pounds per design, can you imagine, and that's just for starters, there might be all sorts of spin-offs—"

Anna seems spinning herself, circling way above our heads. Dad is staring at her as if any minute now she'll whiz out of the window and up into the wild blue yonder.

good times

I can't concentrate at school. I've got one word whirling round every little squiggle and twist of my brain. R-U-S-S-E-L-L. I wonder if he's thinking about me???

I think about him particularly hard in the last double lesson, art. We've got this new young ultra-hip art teacher, Mr. Windsor. I like him a lot and I love all the stuff he tells us about the history of art and women painters and the changing ways women have been portrayed. I normally hang on to his every word and try to impress him, but his voice today is like background buzz on a radio. I can't even get interested when he shows us some Blake watercolors and Picasso paintings of mythical creatures. Magda and Nadine like the Blake triple Hecate of three young women huddled together. Mr. Windsor says she's a goddess of the Underworld, and then he flashes lots more Greek gods at us and amuses us with Muses.

"Now, I want you all to draw yourselves as a mythical creature. Be as inventive as possible," says Mr. Windsor, handing out paper. "You can use black ink and watercolor, like little Blakelets, or paint like Picasso."

Magda and Nadine want to Sellotape our papers together and do a joint Hecate.

"We can all draw her together," says Magda.

"Ellie can do the bodies as she's the best at drawing and then we'll each do our own heads," says Nadine. "You sit in the middle, Ellie, right?"

I hesitate. I don't really want to join up with Magda and Nadine and do the Hecate. I rather fancy the Muse theme.

"Ellie?" Magda's staring at me.

"Ellie?" Nadine's staring at me too.

They're both looking bewildered.

I feel mean. I don't want to hurt their feelings.

"Right, right, who's got some Sellotape then?" I say quickly.

Luckily Mr. Windsor isn't keen on mutual-effort art either.

"No, you three. I know you're inseparable, but I'd sooner you each made a solo attempt," he says.

I pretend to be disappointed like Nadine and Magda, and settle down to my Muse. I get so caught up in it that I don't chatter to the others. I don't even look to see what they are doing. Mr. Windsor comes and has a wander round just before the bell goes to see how our paintings are progressing.

"I like it, Nadine," he says, laughing.

I stop and peer at Nadine's painting. She's drawn herself as a mermaid, her long black hair discreetly veiling her bare top, her jade-green tail wittily tattooed with little navy sailors and anchors and ships.

"What do you think of mine, Mr. Windsor?" Magda asks eagerly, looking up at him and batting her eyelashes. She flirts with any guy, great or small, old or young, gross or gorgeous, but she's always thought Mr. Windsor *seriously* special.

He looks at her painting—and then looks at her like she's seriously special too. I crane my neck to see it properly. I know Nadine is nearly as good at art as me but Magda's only fair-to-middling. Her drawing isn't that good, I suppose—it's just the idea. She's drawn herself as a phoenix, with a fluffy head of feathers just like her own flame-red curls, and she's flying right out of a fire.

"What a great idea, Magda," says Mr. Windsor. "I'm truly impressed. You two didn't just copy an idea like most of the others. You invented your own. We'll have both of these up on the wall. Now, Ellie, let's see what you've been up to."

He stands behind me and is quiet for rather longer than usual.

"How strange," he says at last.

"Strange?" says Magda, coming over to have a look. "Oh, Ellie, it's ever so good. I wish I could draw like that."

"You look just like you—and the artist looks just like a certain boy we all know," says Nadine, giving me a nudge.

"Don't you like Ellie's painting, Mr. Windsor?" says Magda. "I *wish* I could draw like her."

"It's . . . interesting," says Mr. Windsor.

He looks closely at my picture of me posing self-consciously while Russell sketches me. It's very similar to the Picasso he showed us but his model was naked and I'm obviously not going to portray myself without a stitch on. Come to think of it, the artist was naked too, but I'm certainly not drawing Russell starkers. I suddenly wonder what he looks like bare and start blushing.

"Why did you draw yourself as a Muse, Ellie?" Mr. Windsor asks.

I wonder what he's getting at. Does he think I'm pathetic for imagining I could ever be a Muse figure? Perhaps he thinks it deeply sad that a plump plain girl like me could ever inspire anyone to create worthwhile art?

"I know Muses are meant to be kind of beautiful," I mumble. "It was just a bit of . . . artistic license."

"Muses can look any way you want them—but *you're* the artist. You should be the one clutching the paintbrush, not the model staring into space empty-handed."

I think he's paying me a compliment. I suddenly slot back into my senses. I turn my paper over and for the ten minutes left of the lesson I do a quick sketch of Magda and Nadine and me as Hecate—me wearing my glasses and looking earnest, Magda with her head on one side in a flirty fashion and Nadine gazing dreamily into the distance. Magda and Nadine have a happy giggle and Mr. Windsor grins.

"We'll put that one on the wall, OK?" he says as the bell goes. "Home time! Off you go, girls."

He doesn't need to tell me twice. I can't WAIT to see Russell. Nadine's eager to be off too but Magda's hanging about, watching as Mr. Windsor gathers up his stuff and fumbles for his car keys.

"Oh, *sweet*! I like your Teletubby key ring, Mr. Windsor!" she says. "Tinky Winky! Whoops, where's your handbag?"

"You're a cheeky girl, Magda. It's a good job I'm such a laid-back, tolerant teacher," says Mr. Windsor, trying to shoo her out of the classroom.

"You're not like a *teacher* at all. Well, not like Mr. Prescott and Mr. Daleford and Mr. Pargiter. I can't imagine them with Teletubby key rings."

"It's not exactly the coolest of icons," says Mr. Windsor.

"Are they your favorite telly program then, Mr. Windsor? Do you watch it again and again?" Magda asks.

"I'm telling you again and again—it's time to go home."

"You're quoting that little Andy Pandy now. My nan used to watch him," says Magda. "And my mum loved the Clangers. Do you have little kids who like the Teletubbies then, Mr. Windsor?"

"Little kids! I'm not even married. Now, buzz off, the lot of you."

Magda buzzes at last. She practically skips out of the art room and out into the playground.

"Did you hear that, you two! He's not married!"

"Magda! Are you crazy?"

"Magda, you can't go after *Mr. Windsor*!"

"Why not? How old do you think he is? Only twenty-something. That's not really old, is it?"

"You *are* crazy!"

"Anyway, I've got to run," I say quickly. "I'm seeing Russell at McDonald's and I can't bear to be late or he'll think *I've* stood *him* up."

"Oh dear, I'm starting to feel a bit left out here," says Nadine. "First there's you blowing hot and cold over this Russell, Ellie, and now Magda suddenly gone totally bananas over Mr. Windsor. I'm the only sane one left."

"Cheek! Look at the way you were with Liam!" I say. Nadine flinches a little. I bite my lip, wishing I hadn't said it.

"Sorry, Nadine," I say guiltily, giving her hand a squeeze.

"That creep Liam is history," says Magda firmly.

But there at the school gate is Liam himself.

He's standing looking our way, ultra-cool in his black clothes, his hair flopping sexily forward, his dark eyes gleaming.

Nadine is always pale but now she goes so white I'm scared she's going to faint. She takes one wobbly step, then I grab her by the elbow, Magda the other.

"There, Nadine. Don't worry. We've got you," I say.

"The cheek of that creep!" says Magda.

"What's he doing here?" Nadine whispers.

"He shouldn't be allowed to hang round our school," I say indignantly. "We ought to tell Mrs. Henderson."

"Yeah, you know what a fierce feminist she is. She'd take aim with her hockey stick and give him a swift crack right where it hurts," says Magda, chuckling.

Nadine certainly isn't laughing.

"Do you think he wants to talk to me?" she says.

"Well, you're not talking to him!" says Magda. "Don't worry, we'll walk you straight past him."

"Don't even glance in his direction," I say.

But Nadine can't seem to take her eyes off him.

"You don't *want* to see him, do you?" I say.

"Oh God, Nadine, think about the way he treated you. The way he treats all the girls he's been out with," says Magda.

"I know," says Nadine. "OK. We'll walk straight past. Quick!"

We start walking across the playground. Nearer and nearer. Liam is looking straight at us. His blue eyes are boring right into Nadine.

"Take no notice, no matter what he says," Magda hisses.

"Remember Claudie? Don't even think about him. He's not worth it, worth it, worth it," I sing softly.

Nadine takes a deep breath and walks on. She doesn't make a sound but her lips are moving. I think she's muttering Claudie's song under her breath.

We draw close, swinging sideways out the gate, the three of us marching in unison, like we're joined at the hips, a walking manifestation of Hecate.

"Hi, Nadine," says Liam. He ignores Magda and me, like we're Nadine's walking sticks. We do our best to prop her up.

She doesn't say a word. She doesn't even glance in his direction. We walk her past him and hurry her up the road.

"He's still staring after us," says Magda.

"Let's hurry!"

We practically sprint to the corner. Magda peers back breathlessly.

"It's OK, he's still standing outside school. The nerve! Mind you, I do get what you saw in him, Nadine. He's gorgeous. Look at his bum in those jeans!"

"Magda, stop being ridiculous," I snap.

Nadine still says nothing.

"Naddie? Are you all right?"

She gives a little nod.

"You don't *still* have a thing about him, do you?"

"He's history, like Claudie sings," Nadine insists.

"Isn't it good my dad got tickets?" says Magda, quickly steering the subject away from Liam. "They were very nearly sold out too. It's on the twenty-ninth. That's the Friday night. We'll have a great girly night out."

"Yeah, it'll be fantastic. I can't wait," I say.

"Claudie wouldn't waste her time on any guy who used her," Nadine mutters.

"Too right she wouldn't. She wouldn't waste her time." The word *time* makes me glance at my watch. "Oh help! I can't be late. Look, I have to charge off to McDonald's to see Russell. Is that OK?"

"Don't worry, Ellie. I'll go back to Nadine's with her," says Magda. "We can do our homework together, right, Naddie?"

"Oh no, it's maths! Can I copy off you two tomorrow morning before school?" I beg.

"You could always ask Russell for help," says Magda. "Seeing as he's the seriously brainy type."

I'm not so sure I appreciate this remark. I like it that Russell's clever. It's a huge bonus he's so gifted at art, too. But I wish Magda thought he was gorgeous like Liam.

Do *I* think Russell is gorgeous? I try to conjure him up in my mind as I rush off toward the town center. It's weird, I've thought about him constantly all day and yet now when I'm about to meet him I can't really think what he looks like. I just keep seeing my own portrait of him instead.

Then I catch a glimpse of myself in a shop window and I start to worry what *I* look like. If only I'd thought to bring some other clothes with me to school. I look so stupid in my horrible old school uniform. The skirt's so short and my legs are so fat. My hair's standing on end like I'm Shock-Headed

Peter and I've got yogurt slurp all down my school sweater. I put down my schoolbag, struggle out of my blazer and start pulling my sweater over my head. There's a chorus of piercing wolf whistles from a stupid little gang of Year Seven Allen's boys.

I stand my ground and sigh disdainfully, even though I can feel myself going red.

"Hey, girlie, all your blouse is undone—you can see your whatsits!" one yells.

I struggle. I know it's a joke. But I can't be sure. What if . . . ?

I look down. My blouse is buttoned. They all shriek with laughter. I say farewell to dignity, make a very rude gesture at them, grab my gear and hurry on. I'm not at all sure about wearing the blouse without the sweater. The buttons do come undone sometimes. It's too tight so that it bunches across my chest. It doesn't look remotely inviting, it just looks like I've got a couple of unwieldy bags of sugar stuffed down my shirt front. What if I've got all sweaty with the rush and the hassle with Allen's idiots? If only I'd taken my deodorant to school. Oh God, if only I could rewind and start again—but I really need to fast-forward because the journey's taking longer than I thought.

Maybe he'll give up on me or think Dad never passed on the letter? Maybe I almost wish Dad *hadn't* given me the letter. What's the matter with me? I've been looking forward to seeing Russell all day but now I'm dreading it! My hands are clammy, my blouse is sticking to me, my tongue is tingling, my tummy's clenched. I'm dying to go to the loo and my brain is going *bleep bleep bleep*. I can't think. What shall I say when I see him?

Hello, Russell. Hi there. Fancy seeing you. Sorry I'm late. Remember me? Hallo hallo hallo. Knock knock, who's there?

Oh God, I'm really going crazy. I'm going into the Flowerfields Shopping Centre, it's just down the escalator and I'm outside McDonald's and *bang bang bang* my heart beats because I can see him there, peering all round, looking for someone, looking for me.

He sees me and starts waving—so eagerly he knocks his cup of coffee flying. I go up to him, grab a couple of paper napkins and get mopping.

"Typical!" says Russell. "I was sitting here practicing the coolest way of saying hello and then I see you and spill my coffee all over myself. Not exactly the coolest action in the world."

"It's possibly the hottest way of saying hello," I say, discarding one soggy napkin and starting with the next. He's got coffee all in his lap too but I can't really dab at his trousers.

"Good job it's lukewarm because I've been here ages," says Russell.

"I'm sorry I'm a bit late. Did you think I wasn't coming?"

"I wasn't sure. Your dad was really mad at me at first but he didn't seem like the kind of guy who'd hang on to my letter. Though I didn't know if you'd want to come. You must feel I'm totally pathetic—not allowed out by my stupid father. Talk about humiliating."

Russell raises his eyebrows in mock despair and mops his sketchbook dry.

"The coffee hasn't gone on your sketchbook, has it?"

"I don't think so. Maybe it's added a sepia tint or two! I didn't have it open. I didn't want to look too posey, sketching again, even though it's what I like to do best. Well, second best."

"So what's *best* best then?" I ask.

"Kissing you," says Russell.

We both blush violently.

"I'll get you a coffee—and me a replacement," says Russell. "Do you want anything to eat?"

We end up sharing French fries, taking turns chip by chip.

"I can't get over you practically combing the neighborhood for me," I say.

"I'm sorry, it was a kind of desperate needy thing to do."

"I think it was seriously romantic," I say.

"Yeah, like it's seriously romantic not even to be allowed to ask you out just now because my father's such a stupid mean old fart," says Russell. "Well, he can't physically stop me going out and doing what I want. I mean, I'm stronger than him for a start. But he says I can't live there if I don't accept his ground rules. I don't want to go back to living with my mum either, because she and my sister have this all-girls-together thing and all they seem to do is slag off Dad and if I do any totally normal bloke thing like leave the toilet seat up then they go on about me being just like my father, which makes me so mad. It's like there isn't any ideal *home* home. When Mum and Dad first split up I used to shuttle between them, one week with Mum, then I'd pack my little suitcase and go and have one week with Dad."

"I read a book about a girl like that," I say sympathetically. "It must have been really hard on you, Russell."

"Maybe I'm just exaggerating my situation to get you to feel sorry for me."

"OK, you're allowed to do that, just so long as you let me bang on about *my* problem family."

I have a good moan, though I feel a bit mean as Anna has been so sweet to me recently, Dad seems to have taken off his unreasonable Ogre head, and even Eggs has seemed quite cute the past couple of days, drawing lots of pictures of monsters and monkeys and trucks and fire engines, claiming he's helping Anna with her jumper designs.

"I suppose my family aren't *too* terrible," I wind up eventually. "But I can't wait until I'm eighteen. Nadine and Magda and I all want to share a flat. Maybe we'll all go to art college. *Not* my dad's. Hey, show me what you've been drawing."

I'm hoping there are sketches of me. There are *several*! Me arm in arm with Magda and Nadine, me chatting on the bus, me walking hand in hand with Russell in the park. He's glamorized me considerably. He's defrizzed my hair and penciled it in as flowing curls, pared down my weight, added several inches to my height and given my outfit a designer edge. He's set about improving his own image too, adding to his stature and muscle tone until he looks like an Olympic athlete bulging out of his uniform. He's made his hair more sexily floppy and he's given his features a full Leonardo DiCaprio makeover so he could get a job as his double for the movies.

"I wish. You wish," I say, laughing.

"What?" Russell sounds a little peeved.

"We don't look like that."

"Yes we do. Well, *you* do."

"Rubbish! And the park certainly doesn't look a

bit like that. You've drawn it like a romantic rose-strewn bower."

"OK, maybe I used a bit of artistic license here and there. Tell you what, let's go to the park now and I can sketch it like it really is."

"Oh yeah. So it's not 'Come up and see my etchings.' It's 'Come out and watch my sketchings!'"

"You can sketch too. Come on, Ellie, finish up the chips and let's get cracking."

"But you've got to go home and so have I. Look at all the trouble we both got into last time."

"It's not even half past four! I told my dad I was going to this art club—I do sometimes stay on, we've got a great art teacher. Anyway Dad and Cynthia don't get back from work till half past six so he's not to know, is he?"

"My dad is back from art college by five some nights. And Anna will be home with Eggs."

"Can't you say *you're* at an art club?"

"I suppose. Mr. Windsor was talking about starting one the other day. He's great too. My friend Magda's developed this serious crush on him. She was having this terrible flirty conversation with him today—and he seemed to be enjoying it terribly." There's a little pang to my voice. *I've* had a little bit of a crush on Mr. Windsor since he came to our school. I suppose I've always thought of him as *my* Mr. Windsor because I'm the one so nuts on art. But he's never chuckled at me the way he did with Magda.

"Everyone always fancies Magda like mad," I say.

"I don't," says Russell.

"Don't you?" I say, ever so eagerly.

"No, not a bit. I mean, she's fun, she's pretty and all that, but—"

"But?"

"Well. She's a bit obvious. All that giggly wiggly stuff."

"Hey, Magda's my friend," I say—but there's a tiny wicked bit of me that is thrilled.

"I know, I know. You and Magda and Nadine, the Unholy Trinity."

"What do you think of Nadine? She's not giggly and wiggly."

"Yes, but she's sort of weird and stuck in her own world. She's OK, Magda's OK, but you're the one that I want, Ellie."

It's a supremely magical moment—but his words remind me irresistibly of John Travolta. Russell grins, on the same wavelength.

" 'You're the one that I want,' " he sings.

"Oooh oooh oooh!" I sing back, and we both collapse.

We have this long involved old-movie conversation all the way on the bus, comparing our special favorites. Sometimes we differ. He's a total *Star Wars* freak while I find it all a Big Yawn. He wanted to vomit while watching my beloved *Little Women*. I get scared telling him my number-one favorite film is *The Piano*. I won't be able to bear it if he sneers. The relationship between Flora and Ada is just the way I remember it between my mum and me. But Russell says it's one of his favorites too because it's so strange—those poke bonnets and crinolines and the piano on that bare beach are such haunting images. Russell is obviously into film theory. He's predictably a Tarantino fan. He starts the little riff about McDonald's in Europe and he's impressed when I chant along with him. Then we rewind to the start of the movie and do the stickup scene. We get a bit carried away and this little old guy at the front of the bus jumps up like it's *really* a stickup, and a fish-faced middle-aged lady tells us to Mind Our Language.

It's just as well it's my stop next. We're still giggling when we get to the park. We're both hoping it might have turned into the magical glade in Russell's sketchbook, but it's just the scrubby old park, totally unromantic in the daylight, with toddlers howling, mums shouting, an old vagrant muttering, torn Magnum wrappers flapping in the breeze and dog dirt in the grass.

"*Not* a haunting image," I say.

"We'll go over by the trees," says Russell.

But there's a little group of guys, one with his hood up, several looking shifty. There seems to be an exchange of hard cash for equally hard drugs.

"Maybe going over by the trees isn't such a good idea," says Russell. "So where *can* we go?"

We end up walking out of the park and down by the old allotments. Someone has planted cabbages. Their sour reek fills the air. We stand looking at each other, breathing shallowly. It's hard knowing how to start kissing in broad daylight, especially as there are several old chaps and a girl in dungarees digging their allotments. Russell glances round and then closes in on me. His eyes morph into one as his lips touch mine. His head is at a slightly awkward angle so my glasses get pressed into my nose, but then the kiss takes over and my eyes blur and the cabbages turn into great green roses and the shouts and yells sound sweet as birdsong.

"We're going to lose track of time all over again," I say, when we eventually draw breath.

"Who cares?" says Russell, and kisses me again.

"I care," I say eventually. "I don't want you to get into any more trouble with your dad."

"I care too," says Russell. "I don't want you to get into any trouble either. So we'll go now. Well, in a minute. One more kiss."

We do go . . . after quite a few more kisses. Russell sees me right to my front door and we arrange to meet tomorrow. Same time. Same place. Same boy and girl. Same love story.

I waltz indoors, sure that Anna will take one look at my wild hair and shining eyes and flushed face and swollen lips and start to create. But Anna is busy with her own creating, crawling round on her hands and knees on the living room carpet, matching up pieces of sweater, while the kitchen table is covered in potential designs. Eggs is sitting cross-legged in a corner, a huge toffee in his mouth clamping his teeth together. He is also creating, with needles fat as crayons and scarlet triple-knitting wool.

"'ook, 'ook, Ellie," he says, dribbling toffee-slurp down his chin. "I c'n *knit!*"

"Good for you, Eggs."

"I wish *I* could knit," Anna says. "Dear goodness, what have I taken on, Ellie? I must be mad! You wouldn't be an *angel,* would you, and help come up with one or two more designs?"

"How about an angel design then? An angel motif on the front, little gold Lurex halo, wings in some fancy overstitch to look like feathers—and then a little devil on the back with silver Lurex horns and hooves?"

"Oh, Ellie, that's brilliant!"

I help Anna all evening, the good-girl daughter with ultra-amazing original ideas. Dad comes home, pats me on my unruly head and delicately inquires if I've had a brief tryst with Russell.

"In McDonald's, yes," I say.

"Ah! Love amongst the Big Macs," says Dad. "Well, just so long as you're home for tea. Good girl."

I am enjoying this new role no end. Maybe I've finally sussed out a way of having a great time *and* being a Good Girl.

Magda and Nadine seem intent on being Bad Girls. At school the next day they listen to my detailed account of My Meeting in McDonald's with My Boyfriend Russell, but they both seem gently distracted. I'm all set to show off just a little weeny bit at going home time because I have another date with Russell but neither Magda nor Nadine seems interested. They have Other Plans.

Magda hangs back when the bell goes, telling us she has "things to do," and suggests we hurry on homeward without her. We blink at her.

"*What* things?"

"What are you up to, Magda?"

Magda looks shifty. "OK, OK, I'm just going to hang around here until Mr. Windsor materializes."

"Oh, Magda, you are a fool."

"He's a *teacher.*"

"I'm not a fool. I seriously think I could be on to a good thing. And it's great that he's a teacher. Who wants to waste their time with schoolboys?" Then she catches my eye. "Sorry, Ellie! I wasn't getting at you and Russell."

"I know, I know," I say. Though I rather think she was.

Nadine and I can't persuade her to come along with us.

"She's mad," I say crossly. "She's making a complete fool of herself. As if Mr. Windsor would seriously consider a little fling with Magda! He'd lose his job for a start."

"Mmm," says Nadine.

She isn't really concentrating. We go out into the playground. Nadine starts. I suddenly realize what's preoccupying her. Liam is waiting by the gate again.

"Uh-oh," I say. "Don't worry, Naddie. I'm here."

She's not even listening. I look at her flushed cheeks. Maybe she doesn't *want* me here!

"Nadine, don't look at him. Come on."

"What's he *doing* here?" says Nadine.

"Well, it's obvious. He's hanging around trying to get you to go out with him again."

"I loved him so much," Nadine says softly. "He was so gentle, so romantic at first."

"Yes, but look what he was really like. Nadine, are you crazy? Stop looking at him!"

She suddenly gasps.

"What is it now?" I take hold of her arm. She's trembling.

"He's not here to see me," Nadine says. "Look!"

I turn—and see Liam waving to someone. A little blond girl in Year Eight is rushing across the playground toward him.

"Oh my God," I say. "He's the absolute pits. Come *on,* Nadine."

But she pulls away from me, still staring at Liam and the little Year Eight girl. He's kissing her now. He is *disgusting.* He's doing it deliberately to hurt Nadine. And it's working. She's looking absolutely stricken.

"Please, Naddie. Come away."

"I've got to see him," she says.

"*What?* You're mad!"

"Let me go, Ellie."

"Don't be so stupid. Just come with me. Please. I'm begging you."

"He's not going out with her," says Nadine.

She starts walking toward them.

"Nadine!" I yell at her, furious she can be such a fool.

She turns, shakes her head at me and then goes

on walking Liam-ward. I can't stand it. How can she be such a total idiot?

I ought to go after her. I should haul her away from that creep and keep her locked up until she comes to her senses. But she won't listen. And I'm already late. I've got to go into town to see Russell.

I try one more time.

"Nadine, *please*!"

It's a waste of breath. She doesn't even turn round this time. So I tell myself there's nothing else I can do. I go off into town to meet Russell— but my heart's thumping all the time and inside my head there's this horror video playing of Nadine and Liam leaving the sad little Year Eight girl and going off alone together. . . .

Why do I feel so guilty? It's not my fault. I'm not going to think about Nadine anymore. Or Magda. I'm just going to concentrate on Russell.

He's waiting for me in McDonald's.

He's already bought French fries and arranged a few on a napkin so that they spell out *Hi! X X X*. He leans over toward me and I wonder if he's going to give me those three big kisses here in McDonald's—but there are some other Halmer High boys over by the water fountain and Russell quickly veers away from my lips and nods at me instead. I nod back. Russell nods again gratefully, like we're both auditioning for Little Noddy. Then I slide into the seat beside him and snaffle chips and start telling him all about Magda and Nadine and how they've both suddenly gone crazy. Russell listens for a little while but then he starts fidgeting.

"Never mind Magda and Nadine. Tell me about you, Ellie."

So I tell him stuff and he tells me stuff, and we compare the craziest things like our favorite outfits when we were little kids. I had these terrible pink girly leggings with a pink flowery little top that I pretended was my special ballet dancer outfit! Russell had a favorite pair of jeans that he wore every day for months until they fell apart.

Then we talk about our favorite places. He likes fairgrounds and I like beaches and we both love Whippy ice cream. As I've snaffled more cash from Anna I treat us to McDonald's ice cream with chocolate sauce. Then we get on to the wondrous world of favorite chocolate bars, swopping passions. It's as if we're best friends, not just boyfriend and girlfriend. It's just great.

After a while Russell gets a bit fidgety and indicates that it would be even greater if we could enjoy another Love in the Allotment session. I don't want to look too eager so I demur a bit—but I'm quite keen for us to be alone together too. The park is overrun with little kids playing footie but this time the allotments are empty, apart from a homespun scarecrow who waves his stick arms at us. We take no notice. We take no notice of anything else but each other. I don't even think anymore. I just feel.

Then I *do* have to start thinking, because it's feeling so good that I'm losing all common sense.

"No. Russell. Stop it."

He does stop, though he tries hard to persuade me to carry on. I suddenly think of Nadine and Liam and wonder if they're currently involved in a similar scenario. It makes me a little more understanding, though I'm sure Liam is just using Nadine. Then I wonder if Russell is just using me.

"What's up, Ellie?" Russell says, kissing my neck.

"Nothing. Well. I was just thinking about Nadine—"

Russell sighs. "You're always thinking about Nadine. Or Magda."

"No I'm not," I say, although I've gone off on a Magda tack now and I wonder if she's followed Mr. Windsor all the way home and asked herself in for a coffee. Maybe *they* could be similarly entwined on Mr. Windsor's sofa. The thought is so bizarre I burst out laughing.

"What's funny?" says Russell, trying to draw me even closer.

"Nothing. It's just Magda has this thing about—"

"Magda!" says Russell. "See, I'm right. Magda Magda Magda. Nadine Nadine Nadine. You and your girlfriends!"

"Did your last girlfriend have special best friends too?" I ask.

"Mmm," says Russell. He hesitates. "Well, if I'm absolutely truthful . . . No, you'll laugh at me."

"No I won't!"

"You're my first girlfriend."

"Really!"

"Yeah. I mean, I could have gone out with various girls—and then there's the school discos, I've *danced* with heaps of girls there. Hey, Ellie, there's a special big dance coming up because it's the school centenary. They're trying to make it like a June ball at university. You know, a meal, two bands, a bouncy castle, maybe fairground rides. Will you come?"

"Sure! Though what if you're still grounded?"

"Oh, it's not till the end of the month. Dad will have calmed down by then. And we're all expected to go, partner or not. But it would be simply great if you'd be my partner, Ellie."

"Do I have to wear a ball dress, all low cut with a sticky-out skirt?"

"Oh, no. Well, feel free to go for a little low-cut

number. You'd look really terrific. But no sticky-out skirts, just something maybe . . . slinky?"

Me??? I can't stuff myself into a slinky little number, I'd look positively obscene. I mentally riffle through my entire wardrobe and start to panic. I'll have to see if Anna will fork out for something new. But *what*?

I ponder long and hard, though it's difficult to concentrate while Russell is kissing me. After he's walked me home I'm supposed to be settling down to my homework, but I design and discard a dozen different outfits instead. Anna looks over my shoulder.

"They're great designs, Ellie, but they're all far too sophisticated. The jumpers are very much for the under-tens."

Anna is living, eating and breathing jumpers. It's as if her brain is three-ply cable twist. She's wrapped up in her own woolly world and even when she's talking to Eggs or Dad or me you can see the *click click* of knitting needles flickering in her eyes.

I ring Magda to ask her advice about outfits for Russell's dance, but she's out. Her mum becomes anxious. She thought Magda was round at my place.

I ring Nadine, but she's out too. Her mum becomes annoyed. She thought Nadine was round at my place.

Help! I have unwittingly got both my friends into serious trouble. And what on earth are they doing out late? What's *happened*? Is Magda really having a passionate encounter with Mr. Windsor? And what about Nadine? Oh God, I should have tried harder to stop her going off with Liam. What sort of friend am I?

I'm starting to get really worried. Our phone goes halfway through the evening. I rush to answer. It's Russell.

"Russell!" I say, surprised. I *nearly* say "I hoped you were Nadine/Magda"—but this would *not* be a good idea.

"Dad and Cynthia have gone out for a drink so I've got the place to myself," says Russell. "I'm supposed to be doing my maths homework—"

I've still got last night's maths homework. I'll have to copy off Magda again. And then there's French and I didn't do last night's either. . . .

"But I thought I'd much sooner talk to you."

"That's great."

"I wish we were still in the park together, Ellie. I love it when we're together."

"Mmm. I do too."

"You don't sound very certain!"

"It's kind of awkward right now," I say.

The phone is in the living room. Dad is staring at me, earwigging every word, even though Eggs has the television up so loud I can barely hear my-self. Even Anna has stopped crawling round the carpet and has her head on one side, watching me.

"Awkward?" says Russell. "Oh! You mean you've got Magda and Nadine round?"

I don't like his tone. So what if I *did* have Magda and Nadine round?

"No Magda. No Nadine. But Anna and Dad and Eggs are all in the living room," I say.

"What, listening right this minute?"

"You've got it."

"Can't you use the extension?"

"We haven't *got* one."

"Tell you what. I'll e-mail you a message. Can you commandeer the computer?"

"Russell, we haven't joined the real world. Dad's old Apple Mac isn't up to e-mail."

"OK, OK. I know! I'll write you a sweet old-fashioned love letter. How about that?"

"That sounds great."

"And you'll write me one too?"

"OK."

"And we'll swop them tomorrow? In McDonald's?"

"Right."

"See you then."

"Yes."

"Bye for now."

"Bye."

"Bye, Ellie, it's been great talking to you."

"And you."

"You don't mind my phoning?"

"No. Not a bit."

"Tomorrow then?"

"Yes."

"Bye."

"Bye."

"Oh per-lease, put the phone down!" Dad says—but he's smiling.

I do put the phone down—and smile back. I feel this great glorious grin flash across my face.

"He's very keen," says Anna.

"Mmm," I say happily.

"I still don't approve at all," says Dad, but it's obvious he doesn't *really* mind.

Eggs is the only one looking mutinous.

"I don't like this new boyfriend," he declares.

"You haven't met him, silly," I say, picking him up and turning him upside down.

I used to be able to shake him like a beanbag but now it's a real struggle. Eggs is still skinny but he's growing rapidly. It's a weird feeling that maybe one day he'll be towering over me, and there might be enough muscle in those matchstick arms to pick me up and turn *me* upside down.

I get a flash of what it might be like for Dad. He's so used to me being his funny fat little Ellie.

It must be so weird for him now I've started going out with boys.

"I don't want to meet him!" Eggs gurgles, going beetroot red. "Put me round the right way, Ellie!" He kicks at me and struggles.

"Ellie! He'll be sick in a minute," says Anna.

I right him quickly. I've had Eggs puke all down me before and it's not a pleasant experience.

"I like Dan," Eggs says, harping back to this other boy I used to know.

"Russell is a hundred times better than Dan," I say.

"Do you love him, then?" asks Eggs. He stares at me. "*Do* you? Why have you gone all red? Ellie?"

I retreat rapidly to my bedroom. I let the French and history homework go hang. I worry a bit about Nadine and Magda—but most of the time I lie on my bed and dream about Russell.

Do I love him?

I think I do.

I do. I do. I do.

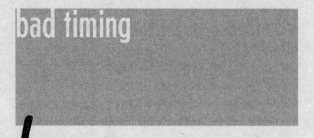

get to school very early. I wait for Magda. I wait for Nadine.

They don't come in early. They're both very late, after the bell. Nadine is very pale, with dark smudges under her eyes. Magda is flushed and jittery, hardly able to keep still. And *she* hasn't done her maths homework, so we're all in trouble.

There's no way we can talk about yesterday evening under the watchful eye of Mrs. Henderson so I pass them both notes.

Nadine—what happened with you and Liam??? Tell me—in detail. Are you OK? You're not cross with me, are you? Love Ellie X X X

Magda—what happened with you and Mr. Windsor??? Tell me—in detail. Are you OK? You're not cross with me, are you? Love Ellie X X X

For five very long minutes I don't think either of them is even going to bother to reply. Then

Nadine starts a note in her Gothic script and Magda writes her little round scribble.

Ellie—I could kill you for ringing my mum like that! I am VERY CROSS with you. I don't want to write stuff about Liam. It was so upsetting and horrible last night. I'll tell you and Magda later. Love Nadine

Ellie—I had a terrible time making up excuses to my mum because you were daft enough to ring up. And I wasn't in the mood. Don't ask about me and Mr. Windsor. It was awful. I'll tell you and Nad as soon as poss. Love Magda

I can't wait to get them round by the Portakabins at break where we can be private.

"Magda! Nadine! What happened last night?"

"You tell first, Magda," says Nadine.

"No. You tell," says Magda.

"I had to go and talk to Liam," Nadine starts. She sees me shake my head. "Don't look at me like that, Ellie. Honestly! You think I'm mad, don't you?"

"Yes! She is, isn't she, Magda?"

"I don't know. Maybe I'm the mad one," Magda mumbles.

"Well, *I'm* not mad," says Nadine. "I don't love

Liam anymore. I hate him. All right, when I saw him outside school I couldn't help feeling a bit funny, especially when I thought he was waiting for me. But then when I saw him with that Year Eight girl—she's called Vicky and she's so *sad*—I just felt boiling mad."

"How dare he treat you like that, deliberately kissing that girl in front of you," I say.

"How dare he treat *her* like that. She's only just thirteen. He is so sick. He was thrilled, too, when I went storming up to him. He looked at me like, *See,* Nadine, look what you're missing. It made me want to slap his stupid face. But I started talking to Vicky, telling her I needed to talk to her privately. She just thought I was making trouble, that I was jealous. Liam tried to make me clear off. But I just stood there in front of them, telling Vicky all this stuff about Liam and how he just uses girls. I came out with all these lovely secret romantic things he once said to me—and of course it turns out he's said exactly the same things to her."

"So then she started to wonder whether I *was* just trying to make trouble like Liam said. I asked her to come for a walk with me so we could have a proper talk together. Liam got very angry then and said I was just jealous because I'd blown my chances with him. He said he wouldn't want to touch me now if I was the last girl in the world. He said holding me in his arms was like holding a marble pillar because I was so stiff, so cold, so unresponsive. He said no boy would ever want to kiss me because I'm so boring."

"How *dare* he, the filthy creep!" I say.

"Don't take any notice of that jerk, Nadine. You're beautiful and all the boys want to go out with you. You didn't take him seriously?"

"Well, it was horrible, him saying all that," says Nadine, her voice shaking. "But it worked for Vicky. She started staring at him in horror, seeing him in his true light at last. So we went off together. We left Liam just standing there. He started yelling stuff after both of us. Vicky started crying. I did too, actually. We went back to her house—it was OK, her mum works late, so we had the place to ourselves, and we could have a good heart-to-heart. It turns out she was all set to do whatever he wanted because he'd got her convinced it was the way to prove her love. I know, I know, it's so sad—but I nearly fell for that old line too."

"Anyway, I stayed really late at Vicky's, because she needed a lot of looking after. I thought I'd tell my mum I was round at your house, Ellie, to save complication."

"Uh-oh. I kind of complicated things more," I say.

"I'll say! When I eventually got home my mum

went bananas. She's convinced I'm seeing this secret boyfriend. It's crazy. All the time I was seeing
Liam she didn't suspect a thing, but the one time
I'm truly just round at a girl's house she goes nuts
and I'm in deep trouble. She's not going to let me
out again in a hurry. She even started on about the
Claudie concert, but I *think* I can still go OK, seeing it's with you two."

"I can't wait to see her on the twenty-ninth,"
says Magda. "The tickets came this morning. The
one good thing. At least the post got me out of
bed. I wasn't going to get up today. I certainly
wasn't coming to school. Not ever again, actually."

"Because of Mr. Windsor?"

"Mmm," says Magda.

"He didn't do anything really awful, did he?"

"I can't believe it. I always *liked* Mr. Windsor."

"He didn't do anything. And *I* like him. He's
lovely. Oh God, I made such a complete idiot of
myself." Magda hides her head in her hands.

"What did you *do*?"

"Tell, Magda! Come on. *I* told," says Nadine,
blowing her nose.

"Mags! You've got to tell us. We tell each other
everything," I say, pulling her hands away.

Her face is as red as her hair.

"OK, OK, I'll tell. I followed Mr. Windsor home
yesterday. I stayed back after school and we had a

little natter about this and that. I made out I was really getting into art and how much his lessons mean to me. He seemed dead chuffed about it. I didn't *mean* it. I know you're stuck on art, Ellie, but it's just a bit of fun to me. Anyway, Mr. Windsor and I seemed to be getting on like a house on fire. The way he was looking at me with those big dark eyes of his it was practically Great Fire of London time! I didn't just want to leave it when he sloped off to his car. I wondered about asking him for a lift but I thought he'd be a bit uncomfortable on the school premises, anyone could be watching. So I thought, OK, cool it for a bit but maybe . . . sort of turn up at his house!"

"Wow! Magda, you really flipped!"

"Tell me about it!" says Magda, shaking her head.

"You didn't *go* to his house?"

"I did. Well, his flat. It's fabulous too, just the way you'd imagine, this big airy loft space in one of those converted warehouses near the river. It's not fair! Why does everything about him have to be gorgeous?"

"How did you know where he lives?"

"You couldn't have run along behind his *car*!"

"How do you *think* I found out where he lives? I looked him up in the telephone directory at home. And I changed out of this ropy old uniform and wore my black lacy top—"

"The see-through one!"

"Well, I had my bra on—and my black trousers, the brilliant ones that kind of show off my bum, and my red sandals with the high heels to show him I don't have to look like a boring little school-girl."

"I'll say!"

"I made out to Mum that you'd set me up with this double date, Ellie, with your Russell and some mate of his. I warned her I might be late back and then I got the bus over to the river—"

"Your mum didn't mind you going out late?"

"Your mum didn't mind you going out all tarted up and glamorous?"

"Mum's reasonably cool about it. She's always trusted me—until *you* phone up, Ellie, and blow the whole thing."

"I wasn't to know, was I? But I'm sorry all the same."

"I know. Anyway, I found the right block for Mr. Windsor and there's this entryphone thing. I hung round for a bit wondering how I was going to announce myself. To be absolutely truthful I very nearly chickened out at that stage. If only I had!"

"Magda, I just can't believe you had the nerve!"

"I must have been completely crackers. OK, I announced myself over his answerphone, sort of 'Hi, it's Magda here.' And then I waited. Mr.

Windsor says on the intercom, 'Magda who?' which didn't exactly help my self-esteem. But then I thought he was maybe acting dumb deliberately to be cautious. After all, there aren't that many Magdas around. I said I was Magda from school. He just said 'Oh!' sounding amazed. I mean, we'd been chatting away only an hour or so before. I wondered if he was ever going to invite me in so I spun him this story about some dodgy-looking guy I thought might be following me, so he buzzed the door release.

"I went rushing up the stairs and there he was, standing by his front door, looking really anxious. He asked all about the dodgy guy and I said it was OK, I'd maybe been imagining it, but could I come in and wait for a bit just to make sure he was gone?

"He still hesitated, looking like he hardly recognized me. I suppose he's so used to seeing me in my dreary old school uniform. He asked what I really wanted. I said I wanted to talk to him. He said maybe I'd better talk to him at school and I said I really needed to talk to him now, so he let me in, though he sort of edged round me and kept well away, as if I had a filthy cold and he was scared of catching it."

"I was really bowled over by his flat. It's ultra-cool, polished bare boards, very minimal chic, not much furniture at all. He had one of those bashed-about metal sculptures in a corner. The walls were the only crowded bit. Paintings. All his."

"What were they of?"

I couldn't help envying Magda terribly. I'd give anything to see Mr. Windsor's flat—especially his paintings.

"I don't know. Women, mostly."

"What, portraits? Full-length? Nudes?"

"Ellie! As if it matters! Get on with the juicy bit, Magda," says Nadine.

"It matters to me!" I say. "What style, Magda?"

"Sort of realistic but a bit splotchy," Magda says vaguely.

"What kind of colors?"

"Darkish. I think. I don't know. I made out I was looking at this one painting—a woman in a blue dress, OK, Ellie?—and I said stupid stuff about it being a happy picture and it made me think of the seaside. It was just because the woman was wearing a sundress and she looked like she had a tan, but it turned out it was a lucky guess because he'd painted it on holiday. He burbled on about the quality of the light, blah blah blah, but I just wanted to know who the woman was, but I didn't like to ask in case it sounded crass. I wish I had, then I could still have got out of there without looking a total fool."

"What did you *do*? I'm going nuts with the suspense," says Nadine.

"So I sit down on the sofa while Mr. Windsor's still nattering on about his old painting and gradually his voice trails away and he asks me why I've come round. So I say, ever so casual, that I was meeting someone else later, but I'd been told he lived in these flats down by the river so I thought I'd just pop by. Like you do.

"He still seemed a bit fazed by this and asked *who* had told me where he lived so I just laughed and wouldn't tell him. Then he asked who I was going to be meeting and I laughed some more and said I didn't want to tell him that either. He went off at a bit of a tangent then, asking me ever so seriously about who I was going out with. I thought he was maybe a teeny bit jealous, which was simply great, so I hammed it up a bit, and he got even more serious and seemed to think that I'd come round to discuss this mythical boyfriend with him. He said perhaps I was getting more involved than I really wanted and though he was flattered I wanted to discuss it with him maybe I'd do better talking things over with some other teachers—like Mrs. Henderson! Dear God, imagine discussing your love life with Mrs. Henderson! So I said—I said—Oh God, I said . . ."

"*What* did you say?"

"I said I wanted to discuss my love life with him. Because *he* was my love life," Magda mumbles, ruby-red.

"You didn't say that!"

"You're kidding, right?"

"I wish I was. But I did say it. I must have been barking mad. Woof woof," Magda says. "It was just I thought we'd be pussyfooting around all evening. Oh help. First it's dogs, now it's cats. I'm going completely batty. There you are. Bats."

"Magda. Calm down. Take a deep breath. And now tell us what Mr. Windsor said!"

"He didn't say anything for a full minute. He just gave me this awful astonished appalled look. Then he kind of paced round the room saying nothing at all while I sat on his sofa wanting to sink straight through the cushions because I could see I'd made this *huge* mistake. Then he went out into his kitchen and I thought this was a signal to me to go so I was just about to make a bolt for his front door when I heard this tinkle of glasses and a pop of a bottle opening and he came back with a Coke for me and a glass of wine for him. He gave me my drink and then he sat down on the sofa too, but right up the other end. Then he says, 'Oh, Magda,' shaking his head. And I take a little sip of Coke, shaking so much my teeth go clink against the glass. I managed to stammer out 'Oh, Mr.

Windsor' and then we both have a silly giggle. Then Mr. Windsor says—oh God, he was so lovely which kind of makes it worse—he says 'I'm very flattered that you've taken such an interest in me, Magda, especially when I know you could have your pick of all the boys.'"

"He said that?" I ask enviously. "Those exact words?"

"Yep. And he went on, 'You don't want to waste your feelings on a boring old teacher like me.' So I dared pluck up the courage to tell him he was the least boring man I'd ever met, and he said I was a very sweet girl to say so, but by next week or the week after I'll be totally fed up with him and I'll just look back on this as a fleeting crush. I said I didn't think so—and then I asked him to tell me why he wasn't interested. Was it just because of the school thing or didn't he like me at all? And he said he liked me a lot, but probably not in the way I meant. He said I was way way way too young to be involved with a guy in his twenties and certainly he'd never be unprofessional enough to have any liaison with any pupil, even in the sixth form, and *then* he said, 'And my girlfriend wouldn't be too happy about it anyway.'"

"He's got a girlfriend?"

"They live together. It's actually *her* flat. She's in advertising and I think she must make a lot of money. He showed me this photo of her. It's not fair, she's gorgeous, this black girl with a face like Naomi Campbell and the most amazing long hair. She's called Miranda and when he says her name his face goes all soft and it's obvious he's crazy about her."

Magda sighs.

Nadine sighs.

I sigh.

"He suggested I stay and meet her. He even asked me to have supper with them but I couldn't face it. So I made out I really did have this date with a boy from Halmer High and then I apologized for making such an idiot of myself. He said, 'Don't worry about it, Magda. We'll both forget this ever happened.' But how *can* I forget? How can I ever face him? Every time we have art I'll have to skulk in the toilets for the whole double lesson."

The bell goes and we go back into school—and there's Mr. Windsor coming along the corridor toward us!

"Oh no!" says Magda. "Quick, hide me!"

We can't drape ourselves around her or squash her up small in our schoolbags so there's obviously no way we can hide her. I link into her arm on one side, Nadine does the other, and we carry on walking up the corridor. Mr. Windsor saunters along like he hasn't a care in the world. When he draws near he gives us all his normal cheery smile.

"Hi, Ellie. Hi, Magda. Hi, Nadine," he says, and then he strolls off.

"Phew!" says Magda, breathing upward so sharply she ruffles her fringe.

"What style!" says Nadine. "He acted like it never happened."

"Maybe it *didn't*," says Magda. "Maybe last night was just a mad delusion on my part. Perhaps I dreamt it all."

"I wish my evening was only a dream," Nadine says sadly.

"But you acted wonderfully. You looked after Vicky and you stood up to Liam and showed him just what you thought of him," I say, giving her a hug.

"You don't think I am all cold and boring, do you?" Nadine says.

"Of *course* not!"

"And boys will like kissing me?"

"Nadine! You just wait and see. I'm sure you'll meet someone very special really soon," I say. "I predict it!"

"Predict someone special for me too, Ellie," says Magda, sighing.

"OK, someone special for both of you. Now cheer up, right? Big smiles!"

Magda bares her teeth at me.

"It's all right for you, Ellie. You've got Russell," says Nadine.

"Yeah, right, I've got Russell. But he's nowhere near as important to me as you two," I say—and I mean every word.

But when I meet up with Russell in McDonald's after school I forget all about Magda and Nadine. Russell's bought me a little present! It's in a little black box. A jewelry box???

I open it, my heart hammering.

"Don't worry, it's not a seriously heavy commitment present. It's not like a ring or anything," Russell says quickly.

It's two little pearly daisy-shaped hairslides, very delicate and utterly delightful.

"I hope you like them," Russell says. "I thought they'd look good in all your lovely curly hair. But don't feel you have to wear them if you don't want to."

"I *do* want to! They're wonderful."

"You honestly like them? I spent ages looking at all this hair stuff. The girl in the shop kept giving me these weird looks like she thought I was shopping for myself and rushed off to Madame Jo Jo's of an evening. Here, shall I help you fix them? I just love your hair, Ellie, it's so springy."

"Kind of exploding-mattress springy—but I'm

ever so glad you like it. I've always hated there being so *much* of it, all frizzy curls. I've always wished I had hair like Nadine's, smooth and glossy and gorgeous, but of course mine couldn't ever go like that. I *could* try having it very short like Magda. Do you think it would suit me?"

"You don't want to look like Magda or Nadine. You want to look like you," says Russell firmly, clipping the slides into place. "There! They really suit you, Ellie. Will you wear them to the centenary dance?"

"You bet! In fact I've got this pearly-gray silky top, I could wear that. It's *sort* of slinky."

"Sounds great! I got the extra ticket today. My dad coughed up the cash. He's mellowing considerably. I've told him all about you. Well, I made out my art teacher is a mate of your art teacher and they were both comparing notes on the brilliance of their pet pupils, et cetera, et cetera. I thought it would go down better than saying we met here. Dad has a seriously weird problem about me hanging out at McDonald's. Anyway, we're all set for the dance on the twenty-ninth."

"The twenty-ninth," I repeat.

Why is that date so familiar? Why do I suddenly feel anxious?

"The twenty-ninth," I say yet again. "That's not a Friday, is it?"

"Yes. Why?"

Oh God. I know why.

"I'm supposed to be going to a Claudie Coleman concert on the twenty-ninth!"

"Oh, Ellie! Can't you go another night?"

"I think she's only doing the one gig."

"Claudie Coleman—the singer with the red hair? Yeah, I like her too. But she's always doing concerts. Couldn't you go another time? Please, Ellie."

"Well, it's just . . . You see, Magda's dad got the tickets specially."

"Magda again."

"Don't say it like that, Russell, please. Look, I can't really back out now and let her down."

"I bet Nadine's going too."

"Yes, she is."

"So, Magda and Nadine can go together. It's not like you're leaving one on her own."

"Yes, but, well, we were all three going to have this girls' night out."

"Oh. So they're more important than me and my dance?"

"No! No, of course not." I'm starting to panic. I was so happy just seconds ago, loving my beautiful pearly hairslides, thrilled to bits that Russell had bought them specially for me. Now I feel the slides are digging directly into my head and I can't think straight.

I take Russell's hand, though I'm extremely conscious of all the kids milling round us in Mc-Donald's.

"Russell. You're *much* more important. You know that."

"Then come to the dance with me, Ellie. I've spent the whole day showing off to everyone that you're coming. I'll look such an idiot if I have to say you'd sooner go off to some concert with a couple of girlfriends."

"It's not just any old concert. I've loved Claudie for ages and I've never had the chance to hear her sing live before. And Nadine and Magda aren't any old girlfriends, either. They're my best ever friends."

"But I'm your boyfriend, aren't I?"

"Well . . . yes, of course."

"And you're my girlfriend and I need you to come to this dance with me. *Please*, Ellie."

"OK, OK! Of course I'll come. I'm sure Nadine and Magda will understand."

Russell gives me a quick kiss right there and then in McDonald's.

Nadine and Magda don't understand at *all* when I phone them both in the evening. Nadine listens while I tell her about Russell and his dance.

"You don't mind too much, do you, Nadine?

You do understand, don't you? You'd probably do the same, wouldn't you? Nadine?"

Nadine says nothing at all though I can hear the sound of her breathing on the other end of the phone.

"Nadine, speak to me!"

"I don't want to speak to you," she says, and puts the phone down.

I ring Magda and tell her. Magda says plenty.

"I can't *believe* you could be so amazingly ungrateful! We decided to go to the Claudie concert specially for you, because Russell had stood you up."

"Yes, but he hadn't *really* stood me up, he wasn't allowed out."

"Yeah, yeah, Daddy wouldn't let him out—which if you don't mind my saying so always sounded a totally pathetic excuse, but that's not the point. The *point* is that my dad got us those three tickets—"

"I'll still pay for my ticket, Mags!"

"My dad got those tickets as a *present*. We were going to have this big girly night out."

"I know, but you and Nadine can still go."

"You bet we'll still go."

"And I can come next time Claudie sings."

"Unless Russell asks you out on a pressing

date—like a Big Mac and a large order of French fries."

"You're not being fair, Magda. It's this very special centenary dance at his school. He's told all his friends he's taking me."

"I'm sure he has. I've heard the way those Halmer High boys talk about girls. Well, if you want to go and be exhibited as the latest notch on Russell's belt, you go for it, Ellie."

"You'd do the same, Magda. You in particular. You're boy-mad." I can't stop myself. "I think that's half the problem. You've had a down on Russell right from the start, because he went after me instead of you." Oh God, what have I said? I take a deep breath. "I'm sorry, Mags. I didn't mean any of that," I say—but she's put the phone down on me.

I can't believe it. Both my girlfriends have stopped speaking to me.

I sniff hard and make for the stairs. Everything is a blur. I suddenly encounter something small and bouncy on the stairs—and scream as a large dagger pierces my ankle. The something screams too, at the top of his lungs.

"Ooow! Ellie, you hurt me! You walked straight into me! You did that on purpose and now look what you've done! You've made me drop all my stitches."

"Look what *you've* done. You attacked me with your knitting needle. Look, I'm bleeding! And you've laddered my best tights too, you little moron."

"Hey, hey, what on earth's going on?" says Anna, running into the hall, a ball of knitting wool caught comically round her ankles.

We both start talking at once, Eggs wailing over his rapidly unraveling scarf and me hopping on one leg staunching the trickle of blood.

"Do calm down, both of you. Eggs, stop that noise! I'll pick up your stitches for you, easypeasy. Why did you barge straight into him, Ellie? He was sitting on the stairs as good as gold. I really *can't* stop now, I'm right in the middle of working out this really tricky design and I'm seeing George tomorrow. Look, you're not crying, are you? It's only a little scratch."

"You wouldn't care if I had needles skewered all the way up and down my legs! Why do you always have to take Eggs's side over everything? It's not fair! Why doesn't anyone understand what it's like for *me*?" I shout, and I rush up the stairs and slam myself into my bedroom.

I have a good long howl into my pillow. When I've got to the choked-up, gulping, badly-in-need-of-tissues stage Anna comes into my bedroom with a box of Kleenex and a cold flannel.

"You could at least knock," I grumble, but I let her mop me up. Then she sits down beside me and puts her arm round me. I hold myself stiff for a moment but then relax and lean against her.

"OK, Ellie, tell me," Anna says gently.

"Nadine and Magda aren't speaking to me!" I sob.

"What's happened? Come on, don't cry so. Don't worry, you'll make it up with them. You'll always be best friends."

"Not anymore," I gulp, and I tell her everything.

"Poor old Ellie. This is big problem time," Anna says when I've gone through the whole thing. "Choosing between girlfriends and boyfriends is always very very tricky."

"It's not fair! Why can't they *all* be friends?" I wail. "I thought Magda and Nadine would understand. I mean, this is a very important dance for Russell. It would be pretty magic to go. And he bought me these little pearly hairslides, look."

"Yes, they're lovely. And Russell sounds lovely too. And, after all, he asked you to the dance first."

"Well. No. Actually he didn't. I arranged to go to the concert first."

"So why didn't you tell him about the concert when he started telling you about the dance?"

"I didn't take in the date. You know what a dilly dream I can be about stuff like that."

"You're telling me! So what are you going to do?"

"I don't know. I didn't realize how horrid it would feel, Magda and Nadine turning on me like this. It's not fair, they *both* put boyfriends first. Nadine did when she was going out with horrible Liam and Magda did when she went out with that creep Greg."

"Ah," says Anna. "So what does that tell you about boyfriends and girlfriends? Boyfriends aren't usually permanent, even though you might be crazy about them at the time. Nadine and Magda and you have a very special friendship. I think that's maybe why all the boys get threatened by it."

"So you think I should turn Russell down?"

"I don't know. It's difficult. I don't think there are any rights or wrongs. Which do you really want to go to, Ellie, the concert or the dance?"

"I want to go to both!" I say. "I want to keep in with Russell and please him. I know the dance means a great deal to him. But on the other hand Magda did suggest going to the Claudie concert to cheer me up—and now she's the one who needs cheering up, and Nadine too. Oh, Anna, I *can't* go to the dance with Russell. Do you think he'll ever understand?"

"No! But you'll just have to try to make it up to him in some way," says Anna.

She sees my expression.

"Not *that* way!" she says, and we both burst out laughing.

dangerous times

It is sad being in the doghouse. I feel as if I've been smacked on the nose, had my bone snatched away and been banished to my kennel. Magda and Nadine don't fall on me with open arms when I tell them I can come to the Claudie concert after all.

"Per-lease. You're not doing *us* a favor," says Magda.

"You'd obviously far sooner go to this dance with the Walking Sketchbook," says Nadine.

I have to breathe deeply and take it. I tell myself that they are my very special girlfriends and their love and support and companionship are of supreme importance to me—even though right this moment I want to slap Magda's smug face and pull Nadine's long witchy hair. But I keep my temper—and their own tempers improve. By the end of the day things are nearly back to normal, and we've all started to plan exactly what we're going to wear to the Claudie concert and how we're going to get there, though we're not quite clear

which dad is going to be roped in to do the ferry-
ing about. I give both Magda and Nadine a quick
hug when we say goodbye, and they both hug me
back hard.

I feel enormously relieved that we're all three
best friends again. But now I've got to tell Russell.

That is even worse.

There's no real way of getting round it. And it's
awful, because the moment I see him at McDonald's he starts chatting excitedly about the dance
and how sad it is that half his mates can't get any
girls to go with them and how great he feels that
he can go with me.

"Don't feel too great, Russell," I say sadly, my
tummy a tight knot. "In fact, get ready to feel ultra-
small. And seriously mad at me into the bargain."

"What's the matter, Ellie? Oh God, you can still
come, can't you? Don't tell me your dad's put his
oar in. He's *got* to let you come."

I see a glimmer of a good way out.

"I'm so sorry, Russell. I'd give anything to come
to the dance with you. But you're right, it *is* Dad."

"Oh no! But he seemed to get to like me after
the first sticky ten minutes. *Why* won't he let you?"

"I think he can remember *his* school dances and
the sort of things that went on," I lie smoothly.
"He's been so strict with me recently, Russell. I've
tried and tried but there's no way he'll budge."

Oh, Dad, I'm sorry. I feel so mean, but it's the only way to smooth things over with Russell.

"How about if I go to see your dad and try to talk him round?" Russell suggests.

"No! No, I think that would only make him worse. And he doesn't know I've been seeing so much of you. No, please don't, Russell," I say, panicking. "Then he'll really clamp down and stop me seeing you altogether. He's already got this total ban on me going out at night."

"But he was going to let you go to that concert," says Russell, eyes narrowing. "Are you sure this isn't all just a mega-excuse to get out of the dance so you can go off with your beloved girly-friends?"

"No! Russell! I don't tell lies," I lie, looking hurt.

"But you *are* still going to the concert?" says Russell.

Why did I ever mention it to him???

"Well, maybe," I hedge. "After all, Magda's dad got the tickets. It would be silly to waste it. And my dad doesn't mind because—because he'll drive us there and then drive us back so he can keep an eye on us all the time."

"How about if he drives you and me to the dance and then drives us back? Then he can keep an eye on us," says Russell.

"I don't think that's quite the same."

"No, things aren't quite the same," Russell says—and I don't like the way he says it.

He doesn't suggest we go to the park. He doesn't suggest we go anywhere. We sit in McDonald's for half an uncomfortable hour and then Russell looks at his watch ostentatiously.

"Gosh, is that the time? I'd better get back. I've got heaps of homework to do tonight."

"You're mad at me, aren't you?" I mumble.

"No, really. It's OK. I understand," he says—sounding like he doesn't understand at all.

"I feel so mean letting you down."

"Well." Russell shrugs. "Maybe I'll find someone else to go to the dance with me."

I feel as if he's slapped me in the face. I stand up, feeling sick.

"Right," I say. "Well. See you."

"Yes. See you," says Russell.

We both know what this means. We *won't* see each other. Ever again.

I try to tell myself that if he can be so mean and petty just because I can't go to his dance then he's really not worth bothering about.

"He's not worth it, worth it, worth it."

That's right. I shall go to the Claudie concert with my two best girlfriends in all the world and we'll have a great time.

It's no use. I wish I hadn't said no to Russell. He *is* worth it. I care about him. I love him.

I go straight home.

I go straight home from school the next day too. There's no point going to McDonald's. Nadine and Magda are sisterly and supportive. It doesn't really help.

In afternoon art the next day Mr. Windsor is still into Myths and Legends. I draw a sad silly Psyche drooping miserably because she can't see Cupid. Mr. Windsor is very complimentary but for once this doesn't mean much. He admires Nadine's Circe too but barely glances at Magda's Venus, mumbling "Very good" and edging past quickly. Magda does her best to maintain her cool but her face is as red as her hair.

She rushes out of class without waiting for us.

"Don't you rush off too, Ellie," says Nadine. "I need you to be there just in case . . . well, you know. If Liam's there."

"Oh, Naddie," I say, giving her a little pat.

But it isn't Liam who's waiting at the gate. It's Russell—and he's talking to Magda.

I feel dizzy. Maybe he's always liked Magda. Everyone else does. Maybe he's asking her out instead of me. Maybe he's asking *her* to the dance!

I grab Nadine's arm.

"It's OK, Ellie," she says, peering over at the wall where Liam used to wait. "He's not there."

"Russell *is*," I hiss urgently. "Only he's chatting up Magda. Hang on to me tight, Nadine. I want to walk right past as if I haven't even noticed them. Nadine, stop staring!"

But I can't help staring too. Magda's smiling at Russell. She's looking right into his eyes and he's looking back eagerly, *hungrily*, like she's the juiciest ice-lolly in the freezer and he wants to lick her all up.

"I can't believe it," I say. "How *could* he?"

"How could *she*? She doesn't even like him. She told me she was amazed you were so dotty about him. She said she thought he was a snotty little creep," says Nadine.

"He's *not* a snotty little creep!" I say, outraged. Then I see him smile at Magda and my stomach turns over. "Yes he is!"

"Look, take my arm, Ellie. Come on, we'll whiz past them quick. You hold your head up high. Don't say a word to Russell—*or* Magda. We're not going to speak to her at *all*. And she's supposed to be your friend!"

Nadine leads me across the playground although my legs have turned to jelly. I wobble all over. I try to set my face in a mold but as we get close up everything threatens to melt and run.

"Ellie?"

It's Russell—smiling at *me*!

The nerve! I walk past, my head high.

"Ellie!"

It's Magda, and she's smiling too.

My eyes sting. It's bad enough that Russell could betray me, but I can't bear it that my best friend Magda could do this to me, and so blatantly too.

"Ellie, stop. Wait! I want to talk to you," Russell says, hurrying after me.

"Well, *she* doesn't want to talk to you," says Nadine, elbowing him out of the way.

"Ellie? Nadine? What's up with you two?" says Magda, dodging round the other side.

"What's up with *you*?" says Nadine. "How *could* you, Magda?"

"How could I what? Here's me doing my best to act like Cupid, helping these two idiots get it together again, and you act like I've done something dreadful!"

I stop. Nadine stops. Magda stops. Russell hovers, while we three girls stare at each other.

"What are you on about, Magda?" says Nadine.

"Russell stopped me as I came out of school and asked me how Ellie was and whether she was still mad at him. He'd hung around McDonald's for hours yesterday and she didn't show, so he wanted

to know if she might be willing to make it up or
had he blown it forever. I said I thought she was
still crazy about him and pretty miserable at the
moment and that she'd be more than willing to
make it up—but then you two sweep past with
your noses in the air, not even speaking. I can't
work out *why*. I mean, don't speak to Russell if you
don't want to, Ellie, but don't take it out on me."

"Oh, Mags," says Nadine. "You'll never guess
what Ellie thought!"

"You thought it too!" I say, weak with relief.

"You thought *what*?" says Magda.

"Nothing!" I say quickly, because Russell is in
earshot. I turn to look at him. He looks at me. I
feel like I'm the ice-lolly now. Melting.

"Go on, you two. Go and enjoy your romantic
reunion. Have a happy little snog in McDonald's,"
says Magda.

"French kiss over the French fries."

"Blush amongst the burgers."

"Cuddle over your Cokes."

"Sauce the ice cream with your sweet talk."

"Froth the coffee with your feverish embraces."

"Shut *up*, you two," I say—but fondly.

They're such sweet friends. And so is Russell.
When we get away by ourselves at last he says he's
really sorry he said he'd take someone else to the
dance.

"I just wanted to hurt you, Ellie. It was stupid. You didn't believe it, did you?"

"Of course I didn't!" I insist. "Oh, Russell, I'm still so sorry I've let you down over the dance."

"Well, it's not like it's this super-cool ultra-great social date. It's just a school dance. It'll probably be a totally sad embarrassing occasion, so maybe it's just as well you're not coming."

"Maybe we could go to some other dance together?"

"Sure. That would be great. Though actually I can't dance very well. I sort of fling my arms and legs around and look like a total prat. Maybe if you saw me you'd go off me instantly. Always assuming that you're *on* me, of course."

"You're the one who went off me. You were really mad at me last time."

"You were the one who didn't turn up at McDonald's. I waited *hours*."

"You didn't suggest meeting there. I didn't think you'd go. I didn't think you wanted to see me again."

"I do."

"I do too. Want to see you."

"Oh, Ellie." Russell suddenly pulls me close, right there in the street.

I don't care who's watching. I fling my arms round his neck.

There's a toot on a car horn.

"Eleanor Allard!"

Oh my God! *Mrs. Henderson* is leaning out of her car window.

"Put that boy down at once!" she calls, and then she winds up her window and drives off.

"Uh-oh!" says Russell sheepishly. "Who was that? One of your mum's friends?"

"Mrs. Henderson's my form teacher," I say, hoarse with shock.

"Your *teacher*? Wow, she's a good sport."

"I suppose she is," I say.

But the next day Mrs. Henderson gives me a half-hour lecture about decorous behavior out in the street in school uniform. I am very glad she didn't come across Russell and me later on by the allotments!

"So you're all lovey-dovey with the Walking Sketchbook again?" says Nadine.

"Don't call him that, Naddie, his name's *Russell*," I say, nudging her. I give Magda a nudge too. "What's all this about you calling Russell a snotty little creep?"

"*Me*?" says Magda, all outraged innocence. "Look, I'm the Cupid who brought you two together again."

I can't believe how good it feels to *be* together again with Russell. And with Magda and Nadine.

"I'm so h-a-p-p-y, hippy hoppy happy," I sing in the shower on the day of Claudie's concert. It's this silly little song she's tacked onto the end of her album. It goes on: "*I don't need the love of a good man, I don't need the love of a bad man, I don't need the love of a-n-y man at all—'cause I'm so h-a-p-p-y,* etc., etc." But that's not the way *I* sing it. I invent my own version: "I *do* need the love of a good man, though I don't need the love of a bad man, I do need the love of MY man Russ-ell—cause I'm so h-a-p-p-y, hippy hoppy happy . . ."

The shower is full on so I don't think anyone can hear me. I am wrong.

"I'm so d-i-r-t-y, dippy dotty dirty," Dad bawls from the other side of the bathroom door. "I *do* need the scrub of a good soap, I do need the the scrub of any kind of soap, I do need the scrub of a-n-y soap at all—'cause my daughter's in the shower and she won't let me in so I'm so d-i-r-t-y, dippy dotty dirty!"

"*Dad!*" I say, emerging blushing in my bath towel. "Do you have to listen?"

"*Ellie!*" says Dad, gently pulling a lock of my wet hair. "Can I *help* listening when you're singing fit to bust, O Daughter Diva of the Shower Stall? But hey, I'm glad you're happy. Now what are the plans for the concert tonight? Is Nadine's dad driving you or Magda's? I'm sorry I've got this stupid meeting at the college."

"Magda's dad's taking us," I say.

"Poor guy," says Dad gratefully. "I owe him."

But when I get to school Magda says her dad can't manage it after all because the wheel shaft went on his car last night and it'll need to be in the garage for a couple of days.

We look expectantly at Nadine.

"Oh help," she says. "Dad always takes Natasha and Mum to their loopy line dancing on Friday nights."

"Well, my dad's got this meeting and needs the car so Anna can't drive us. She's stuck with Eggs and she's knitting nine hundred and ninety-nine stupid sweaters every evening anyway," I say.

We ponder.

"Tell you what," says Magda. "We'll take ourselves. Train and then tube. Couldn't be simpler."

"Couldn't be *harder*," says Nadine. "My mum won't let me."

"I don't think Anna will either," I say. "Well, getting there's OK. It's coming back late at night. Won't your mum mind, Mags?"

"Sure. But she won't know. She thinks your dad's taking us, Ellie. Your folks think Ellie's dad's taking us too, Nadine. And Ellie, you can say *my* dad's taking us. Then they don't have to worry and we can push off and have fun."

"Great," says Nadine, though she looks worried.

"Perfect," I say, though I'm fussed about having to tell a whole load of lies all over again.

"So it's all settled," says Magda. "We'll meet up at six, right? At the railway station. Don't worry about cash, Ellie, you can borrow off me. It'll be fantastic. A *real* girls' night out."

So that's exactly what we do. Nadine's at the station first, looking great in black, with new black shoes with huge heels so that she's taller than ever.

"I'm going to have to carry a little collapsing ladder and clamber up it every time I need to talk to you," I complain. "You make me feel littler and dumpier than ever."

"Don't be daft, Ellie. You look great," says Nadine.

I've certainly done my best, trying on half my clothes before plumping (horribly ominous word) for my black trousers and silver-gray top. I suppose I *do* look plump. If *only* I was lithe and long and lean like Nadine. But at least Russell doesn't seem to mind. He phoned me when I was getting dressed.

"I'm just phoning to wish you a good time at the concert," he said.

"If I ever get there. I can't decide what to wear. I'm half in and half out of my trousers at the moment."

"Oh help. You'd better not tell me any more, you're dangerously inflaming me."

"Calm down, Russell, it's not a pretty sight."

"You're a *very* pretty sight. I think you look wonderful in your trousers—and even more gorgeous *half* in them. *Which* half?"

"Oh shut up. Though you're very sweet. I'm wearing your hairslides. They're really great. You're really great, Russell."

There was a sudden totally disgusting mock-vomiting sound. Eggs had crept up behind me and was groaning and gagging.

"Ellie? Are you OK?" Russell sounded alarmed.

"I am fine. However, my little brother, Eggs, is going to be minus his head in a millisecond," I said. "Anyway, enjoy the dance, Russell. I'm really really sorry I'm not going with you."

"I know exactly where you're going to go with me to make it up to me," he said, chuckling mysteriously.

"I'll go anywhere with you, Russell," I said— provoking Eggs into such an orgy of mock-vomiting he nearly made himself really sick.

I didn't tear his head off his shoulders. I felt so great I just laughed at him.

I feel great now. I don't care if I *look* great (as in enormous).

"I'm so h-a-p-p-y," I sing again, and Nadine harmonizes with me. We're not feeling quite so harmonious after another ten minutes have gone by. Magda still hasn't turned up—and she's got the tickets for the Claudie concert.

"Why is she *always* late?" I say.

"Maybe she's got distracted chatting up some boy," says Nadine. "You know what she's like."

"How about you, Nadine?" I ask gently. "Are you over Liam once and for all now, ready to do some chatting up yourself?"

"Sure," says Nadine firmly—but when a boy with dark hair and wicked eyes comes sauntering out of the station, his arm round some girl, Nadine's head jerks and she turns white.

I look at the boy too.

"It's not Liam," I say.

"I know. I just thought it might be," says Nadine.

"Oh, Naddie. You know exactly what he's like now. You've got to forget about him. You'll meet someone else soon."

"I don't think I'll ever meet anyone like Liam," says Nadine. "Not that I'd want to, of course."

I hope Nadine means it. She looks a bit down, so I change the subject.

"Where is Magda?" I say. "Why does she always do this to us?"

"Hi, you two!"

It's Magda, running wiggle-waggle up to us in her high heels, coyly waving to two grinning boys who are eyeing her up and down.

"Sorry! Am I a bit late?" Magda asks infuriatingly. "It was just Warren came round to borrow a tie from one of my brothers and you know I've always had a bit of a crush on him—he used to be at school with my brother, right?—hey, you should see his hair, he's got this totally cool new haircut so he looks a total dish, and this evening when he saw me all dressed up to go out to the concert it was like he'd suddenly seen me for the first time. I wasn't just this silly little schoolgirl. And you'll never guess where he's going tonight! Would you believe he's got this scholarship to Halmer High sixth form and he's going to the dance. And guess what again—he broke up with his girlfriend a couple of months ago and so he was all set to go by himself but when we got talking, Warren and me, he asked if *I'd* like to go to the dance by any chance! Get that! I was ever so tempted actually."

"*What?*" I say.

Magda grins. "But then I thought to myself, it wouldn't be sisterly. I explained I couldn't possibly let my girlfriends down. He was ever so disappointed but said he understood. And guess what yet again—he's asked me out tomorrow night. A real date, a special meal out, at the Terrazza, you know, that Italian place. It's ever so posh. Bit of a change from a burger in McDonald's, eh?"

"Lucky old you," I say a little sourly.

"Yes, you don't have to go *on* about it," says Nadine. "Have you remembered the Claudie tickets?"

"Of course I have. Cheer up, you two! It's our girls' night out, right?"

We do cheer up on the train, messing around and singing Claudie songs. We get on the wrong tube at Waterloo and have to catch another tube back to where we started, and then we bump into some silly middle-aged business blokes and get a fit of the giggles, and then we're not quite sure where to go when we get out of the tube station and we wander round for a while until Magda chats up a policeman and he escorts us all the way up the road.

Time is getting on and we're all starting to worry we might miss the beginning of the concert. I want Magda and Nadine to run but it's like they're both on stilts with their high heels so we don't make much progress. We turn into the main street and see lots of people wearing Claudie T-shirts, which is reassuring—until we realize they all seem to be walking *away* from the concert hall.

"What's up? Where are you going? Isn't the Claudie concert this way?" Magda asks a group of girls.

"She's canceled it," says one girl miserably.

"What? Why? Is she sick?"

"Sick in the head, more like," says another girl, looking angry.

"What are you on about?" says Nadine.

"What's the matter with Claudie?" I ask.

"She's got this boyfriend, right? It was all over the papers last month. Some yobby football player not good enough to kiss her fingertips," says a third girl, pulling at her Claudie T-shirt in distress so that Claudie's image lengthens into a comical grimace.

"So? It's not a crime to have a boyfriend. It's Frankie Dobson, isn't it? I think he's pretty tasty myself," says Magda.

"Oh right, so I suppose *you* think he's just being all masterful now he's told Claudie she has to quit singing," says the T-shirt girl.

"She has to *quit*?"

"Because *he* says so?"

"But *why*?"

"He went to her concert in Manchester last

night and it was a big success. One of my friends was there and she phoned me up and told me all about it. The hall was packed out with fans, and Claudie sang all her most popular numbers, the really stirring stuff. Everyone cheered their heads off. This stupid Frankie couldn't take it. He thought all the songs were an insult to him because lots of them are about independence and women not needing men, so he gave Claudie an ultimatum. If she didn't pull out of her concert tour and stop singing all her very best songs he'd leave her."

"So why didn't she tell him where to get off?" says Magda.

"Exactly! But astonishingly she said he meant so much to her that her career wasn't anything without him."

"Claudie wouldn't say that!" I protest. "She's a total feminist icon. It would go against absolutely everything she's ever sung about."

"That's what *I* thought—even though it was front-page news in the tabloids this morning. So we came along to the concert hoping it was all some stupid rumor, even a publicity stunt. But it's true. The concert's off. She's pulled out the whole tour, just like he said."

I still can't believe it. We go to the concert hall to see for ourselves. There's just little stickers on every Claudie poster saying "Canceled due to illness."

"Perhaps she really *is* ill," I say, because Claudie is my heroine and I'm word perfect in every song and I've taken on board everything she's ever said and I feel as if she's deliberately let me down.

But when Magda goes to the ticket office to try to claim a refund the guy behind the desk confirms everything those other girls said.

"You'll have to write in for your refund. Claudie's left us in the lurch and we haven't got enough cash to give out to everyone. The girl's crazy, wrecking her career for that Frankie. He can't leave the girls alone. He'll be off with some new trophy blonde before Claudie has time to turn round and then where will she be?"

"How can she do this to herself?" I say, practically in tears.

"Cheer up, Ellie. We'll find you someone else to go crazy about," says Magda.

"What are we going to do now?" says Nadine. "I want to listen to some music. There must be something else on somewhere."

"How about coming to listen to us?"

We all spin round. There's a group of boys looking at us, reasonably hip guys, though one's very Gothic, with long black hair and chunky silver jewelry. Nadine stares at him, dazzled.

"So, like . . . you're a band?" Nadine says.

"Sure."

I'm *not* so sure.

"Come on, Nadine," I say—but it's a waste of breath. Magda's smiling too, her head on one side.

"A band, eh?" she says. "What are you called?"

"Well, we've gone through a lot of changes. We're just this little indie band at the moment. We've toyed with the name Indie, because I'm Dave and he's Ian and he's Ewan so we're almost there with our initials. I'm lead guitar, he's bass, and Ewan's the drummer. We just need to find some guy called Neville or Neil or something to be the lead singer." He looks at Nadine. "Or a girl, of course. Called Nadine."

Yuck! I can't *believe* his corny old chat-up line—but Nadine seems to be falling for it. She's tossing her hair and looking up at him through her long eyelashes.

"Are you really looking for a singer?" she says.

"Sure! So why don't you come back to my place and have a little jam session with the band?"

"I can't sing!" says Nadine.

Too right she can't. I stand next to her in singing lessons so I should know.

"I can sing OK," says Magda.

"So you come too, Scarlet," says the fair guy, Ewan the drummer.

"What's your singing like, then, babe?" says Ian, the bass guitarist, looking at me.

I can't stand guys who call you *babe,* like you're the pig in that sweet little kids' film. Ian looks a bit like a pig himself, with a snub snouty nose and a bit of a belly.

"We've got to get home," I say firmly. "Come on, Magda. Come on, Nadine."

Magda shrugs and waves at the guys—but Nadine is still staring awestruck at Gothic Dave.

"I like your rings," she says, nodding at the big silver skulls.

"Do you want to try one on?" he says, offering it to her.

"Wow! It's wonderful. I'd give anything for this sort of jewelry," says Nadine.

"I've got all sorts back home, crosses and stuff. Come and see. And we could try out your voice. You certainly *look* the part, doesn't she, you guys?"

Nadine looks pleadingly at me. "Shall we, Ellie? Just for a little while?"

I shake my head at her, astonished.

"Go on. Our van's just round the corner."

"My van," says Ewan, as if he thinks we'll be impressed. He looks hopefully at Magda. "Dave's gaff is only ten minutes away. You'll come, won't you?"

Magda's starting to see sense now. "Maybe not,

fellows," she says. She links into my arm and jerks her head at Nadine. "Come on, Nad."

Nadine looks at us. She looks at Dave. She nibbles her lip, hesitating. She looks down, her long hair falling over her face.

"Nadine!" I say.

"You do what your mates tell you, do you, Nadine?" says Dave, and he gently pushes her hair back so that he can see her face.

"Not always," says Nadine, going pink. "I'll come to your place then, Dave." She stares defiantly at Magda and me. "How about if I meet you back at the station at eleven, OK?"

We stare at her as if she's gone completely crazy. Is she really serious? She's willing to go off with these three complete strangers in a van???

"Nadine, please," I hiss—but I know just how stubborn she can be. And she's always been so mad about weird indie bands. I suppose this is like her dream come true. Only she can't see that it could easily turn into a nightmare.

"We can't let her go off in this van on her own," Magda whispers to me. "She's totally nuts. We'll have to go with her to make sure she's all right."

"Oh, Mags, this is crazy."

"I agree! But if we can all stick together we should be OK. Well, sort of."

"Magda!"

"It's kind of a chance of a lifetime, though, isn't it? I mean, suppose they eventually make it big. And Nadine gets to be the lead singer. Or . . . or me."

I don't know what to do. They've both gone completely loopy. Nadine's already walking off with Dave Skull, and Magda's smiling at Ewan drummer, asking him where his van is parked. I ignore Piggy Ian and slope after the others miserably.

The van is an awful old thing, really bashed in and filthy dirty. Magda looks a bit put out and even Nadine wavers. I grab her quickly.

"Nadine, we can't go in that van with them. We haven't got a clue who they are," I whisper at her.

"We do know who they are. They're these guys in this band," says Nadine.

"They're probably making it all up. And even if they have got a band they'll never let you sing in it, idiot."

"I don't see why not," Nadine says, looking hurt. "Anyway, I want to see all Dave's stuff. Isn't he fantastic? I'm crazy about him."

"You've only been talking to him two minutes!"

"Look, Ellie, you were the one telling me I'd meet someone special soon! You predicted it!"

"Yes, but I didn't predict you'd let yourself get picked up by a complete stranger!"

"You did. With Russell."

"That's different. *He's* different."

"Exactly. He's a silly little schoolkid. These guys are amazing," says Nadine.

I don't know how to get through to her. What little brain she has seems to have shrunk to pea size, rattling round in her obstinate skull like the silver ones grinning on the Dave guy's fingers. He's got hold of Nadine now.

"Come on, babe," he says, and he holds open the back door of the van for her.

She smiles up at him—and climbs inside.

Magda shakes her head up at me. "We'll have to go too," she says.

"I know. But it's mad. *We're* mad if we go."

"Come on, Scarlet! In you get," says Ewan, brushing his fair hair out of his eyes. I suppose he's quite good-looking if you like that type. Magda's starting to look like she does.

"Maybe it's time to live a little dangerously," she says, and she gets in the van too.

So I follow them and get in the van, though I know this is a BIG mistake.

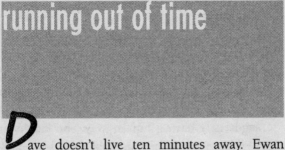

*D*ave doesn't live ten minutes away. Ewan drives for at least half an hour. I haven't got a clue where we are. I can't believe this is happening. Magda is reasonably OK because she's sitting in the front of the van with Ewan and he's got to keep at least one arm on the steering wheel. But I'm in the back with Ian and Nadine and Dave.

Nadine and Dave start acting like a couple almost straightaway. Nadine's proving she's no marble pillar. I don't know where to look. I definitely *don't* look at Ian.

He doesn't seem very interested in me—and yet when I fall against him as Ewan rounds a corner too sharply he hangs on to me, trying to pull me close.

"Don't!" I say, trying to wriggle away.

"What's up with you? I only want to be friendly," he says.

"I don't want to be friendly! I'm in a relationship already," I say primly.

"So? I am too. Come on. Let's get cozy, eh?"

"No thanks!"

"OK. Be like that. You're just a silly little kid. Why can't you be more like your mates? At least they're having a bit of fun."

What a *pig*! I imagine his snout rootling in the mud, his big pink pig-belly smeared all over.

Magda isn't having fun anyway. She laughs at stuff Ewan says but then she looks suddenly outraged and flounces away from him, as he's obviously gone too far.

Nadine's starting to look worried too. She keeps trying to wriggle free.

"Where on earth are we?" she says desperately. "We've been driving ages."

"We're very nearly there. Just around the next corner," says Dave Skull.

And the next and the next and the next. And then eventually Ewan slows down and we drive slowly through a seedy council estate with boarded-up shops, overflowing dustbins and a few scraggy boys sucking on cans of lager like babies with bottles.

"We're here," says Dave.

"Here?" says Nadine, staring out, dazed. "You don't live *here,* do you, Dave?"

For the first time in her life she sounds just a little bit like her mum.

"What's up, sweetheart? Don't you like life when it's a little on the wild side?" says Dave. "Come on, out you get."

Magda and I look at each other, trying to work out what on earth to do now. Nadine is whiter than usual, her lipstick smeared all over her chin.

"Oh help," she whispers. "Maybe this wasn't such a good idea after all."

This is the scariest place I've ever been. The boys drinking lager yell ugly stuff at Magda when she wriggles out of the van. She reacts with her fingers but this just encourages them.

"Hey, clear off, you berks," says Dave Skull. Well, that's *approximately* what he says. He's got hold of Nadine again so she can't run away. He can see she's having second thoughts. Third, fourth, fifth thoughts.

"I didn't realize it had got so late," Nadine says. "I'm sorry, but I think we really ought to get back now."

"We'll take you back. Later on. Let's go and play a little music, eh?"

"I can't sing at all, actually," says Nadine.

"Never mind. I'm sure you can dance. I'd like to watch you dance, Nadine."

"Yeah, sure you would," says Magda. "Look, we have to get back. Now."

"Keep your hair on, Scarlet," says Ewan. "We'll take you back. Later. Come and strut your stuff first. We want to hear you sing too."

"I'm not in a singing mood anymore," says Magda.

"Then we'll have a little drink first. Loosen you up. Yeah, we'll have a little party, right, Dave?"

"You bet."

"You're on," says Pig Ian.

We look at them. They look at us.

"OK, just one drink," says Magda.

"No!" I whisper. "Let's just run off, please!"

But Magda's looking round at the guys, at the boys drinking lager, at the bleak stone walkways.

"If we try to make a run for it now they'll catch us and then they might get really ugly. We'd better go with them and then clear off as soon as we can," Magda mutters.

"I'm sorry," Nadine wails. "It's all my fault."

"What are you girls whispering about, eh?" says Dave. "Come on. Follow me."

So we do, because there doesn't seem to be any other alternative. They take us in a stinking lift up to the top floor, swooping up so fast I feel sick. It's a relief to step out into fresh air but the view over the balcony makes me dizzy. I hold the rail tight, little flecks of rust embedding themselves in my palms. The buildings below don't look real. I feel

I could jump from roof to roof as if they were stepping-stones.

"Quite a view, isn't it?" says Ian Pig, standing close behind me.

I try to shuffle away from him, pressing against the cold concrete. Space whirls in front of me. I look down down down at the tiny toy world below. The pig rootles nearer. Blood starts drumming in my head. My knees won't lock to hold my legs straight. He puts his damp hands on my shoulders, gripping tight. I give a little squeak.

"Scary, eh?" he says. "Don't worry, I'll keep you safe."

"You let her go!" says Nadine, looking wretched.

"He's only teasing," says Dave Skull. "In you come, then."

I suppose we were hoping it might be better inside. Maybe painted black like Nadine's own bedroom, with Gothic decorations and silver candlesticks and weird posters. But it's just a bleak bare wreck of a flat, smelling of drink and cigarette smoke.

"Hey, no one pretended it was House Beautiful," says Dave, seeing our faces. He's picking up a ropy old guitar—but his strumming doesn't sound very skilled.

"Are you going to sing, Nadine?" he says.

She shakes her head nervously.

"How about you, Scarlet?" says Ewan, sitting on the sofa and slapping his knees as if they were a drum kit.

"Somehow I'm not in the singing mood," Magda says.

"Sure—but we'll fix that," says Dave, nodding at Ian. "Get us all a drink, eh?"

"Just one," says Magda. She's looking at the door, obviously wondering if it might be better to make a dash for it as I suggested.

Dave Skull sees she's looking at the door too. He stops strumming, strolls down the hall, takes out his key—and double-locks the door. Then he puts the key in the pocket of his jeans, grinning.

So this is it. We're really trapped now. Nobody knows where we are. Our families think we're at the Claudie concert and we're being driven home afterwards. They won't worry about us for hours. And what can they do when they eventually phone round and find out we're missing? How can anyone ever find us? We don't even know where we are.

I still feel sick. I wonder if I'm actually going to throw up. I mutter something about needing the loo and find the right door. I flop inside the dank little room, desperately trying to think what to do. If only we were at Claudie's concert enjoying our girls' night out! This is all a crazy nightmare and it's getting worse and worse and worse.

I join the others in the dingy living room. Ian Pig has got his guitar now but they're certainly no real band. They've opened up some cans of beer. Magda and Nadine are clutching a can each.

"Come on, girls, drink up," says Dave Skull. He tosses me a can of beer too. I hold it helplessly.

"What's up? Don't you like the taste?" he says. "I know what you might like more." He brings a bottle of vodka out of a cupboard. "Here, have a little swig of that. It'll help you relax." He passes it to me.

"I don't drink, actually."

All the boys laugh unpleasantly.

"This one doesn't do much," says Piggy Ian.

Ewan tries to pull Magda onto his lap. She bats him off fiercely.

"Maybe this is a big mistake," he says. "They're just silly little schoolgirls."

"My Nadine's cool, aren't you, babe?" says Dave. "Hey, you want to see the rest of my jewelry? Come through here." He gestures toward the bedroom.

"I think I'm OK here, thanks," Nadine says in a tiny voice.

Dave hands the vodka to her and she takes a little swig and then chokes.

"I'll have some too," says Magda, taking the bottle.

She doesn't drink a drop, keeping her lips tightly closed as she tilts the bottle up in the air. "There!" she says, wiping her mouth as if she's just downed a triple measure. "That's better. Hey, how about you guys putting some music on your CD player? Then we can all play and sing along, and we won't feel so self-conscious."

It helps a little to have the music blaring. The three guys down their beers and pass the vodka round. We pretend to swig from the bottle too. Magda's doing her best to lighten things up. Nadine keeps trying to edge away from Dave Skull.

"Hang on," he says, going to his bedroom. He brings back a little bag. Oh God. Drugs.

"Yeah, great idea," says Nadine.

I stare at her in horror—but she gives me a little wink. It's just a quick flicker of her eyelid but it's enough. Magda's watching too, and gives a nod. We watch while Dave Skull and Ewan Drum and Ian Pig start rolling special cigarettes. Dave lights his, takes a deep drag, and then passes it to Nadine.

"Cool," she says, getting up. She wanders over to the window. "This is such a great view," she says, turning her back as she stares out. She seems to be taking a deep drag but I think she's bluffing. Magda joins her at the window.

"My turn," she says, pretending to take a drag herself.

Before I can join them Pig Ian is by my side.

"Don't say you're not into a little light relaxation, Miss Priss," he says.

I giggle foolishly, trying not to antagonize him.

"Here, I'll show you how to do it," he says, taking the roll-up from Magda and waving it in front of me.

"Sure. Great. In a minute," I say, jumping up. "I've just got to go to the loo."

"You've only just been. What's the matter with you?" he says, taking a long drag himself.

"I've got a little bug," I say. "I'll be right back."

I go out into the hall and stand in the loo again, trying to think of some way we can get out. I look up at the window. It's too high up, too small. Much much too small. I could stand on the toilet but I could only get my arm out of the window. My head wouldn't fit through, let alone my body. But . . . maybe we could get out of another window?

I creep out of the loo and tiptoe across the hall to the kitchen. There are two large windows above the blocked sink. One hitch up onto the draining board. I could make it. And Nadine. And Magda.

I think.

I run the water tap. I splash it on my face. I throw cold water over my lovely pearl-gray shirt. Then I take a deep breath and call.

"Magda. Nadine. Can you come out here and help me a minute?"

Pig Ian comes out. "What's up with you, Little Priss?" he says blearily. "What are you yelling for?"

"Oh please, don't look at me. I've been sick," I say. "It must have been the vodka. I don't want you to see me like this, not till I've cleaned myself up. I need my friends. They've got tissues and stuff."

"God, you really are a kid," says Pig Ian disgustedly. "OK, OK, I'll get your mates."

He goes—and Nadine and Magda come running.

"Have you been sick, Ellie?" Magda says.

"This is all my fault," Nadine weeps.

"Shhh! Quick! Shut the door. We'll get out of the window," I whisper.

"Wow!"

"Great thinking!"

"Easier said than done," I gasp, hooking my leg way up onto the draining board and trying to heave myself up after it.

Magda gives me a push, Nadine gives me a shove, and I'm suddenly up on the draining board. I grab hold of the window handle. The whole window frame is rotting and at first it sticks. I pull and tug at it, hurting my hand, and then take off my shoe and give it a last desperate bang. It moves—and the window opens.

Nadine is already up beside me, and she helps haul Magda up.

"Oh help!" I say. "It's a long way to jump. We're all going to break our legs."

"I'd sooner break my *neck* than stay locked up with those creeps," says Magda, and she jumps first. She lands like a little cat, not even tottering in spite of her high heels. Nadine goes next, arms and legs kicking out wildly. She ends up on her bottom but manages to scramble up again unhurt.

My go. Oh God. I stare straight out into empty space. What if I misjudge my jump, leap a little too far, and hurtle right over the balcony?

I clench my sweaty fists.

"*Quick,* Ellie," Nadine whispers.

"Jump like Mrs. Henderson says. Bend your knees and spring," Magda calls.

I jump. I bend. I don't exactly spring. I stumble and hobble and trip. But I'm down, safe on the cold concrete walkway.

"Right, let's get out of here," says Magda, pressing the lift button.

"At least they're all pretty wrecked. It'll take them a while to react," says Nadine.

"Come *on*, lift," I say, jabbing at the button. Nothing happens. We keep peering round desperately at their door. They'll be after us any minute.

"I think we'd better make a run for it, down all the stairs," I say.

So we run along the walkway, making for the staircase. Something feels funny. I'm all uneven, hobbling sideways. Did I twist my ankle? Then I realize.

"My shoe! I left it in their kitchen!"

"Well, we're not going back for it now," Magda gasps.

"They were my best shoes from Shelley's," I moan.

"I'll save up and buy you a new pair, Ellie," Nadine puffs. "And I'll buy you some too, Magda. Name your pressie! Anything to make it up to you."

"Shall we try the lift again on the next floor down?" says Magda.

"But what if they've got into it up at the top?" I say.

"Help, yes! OK, well, down we go."

Down and down and down and down. My tights are already ripped. My foot gets sorer each time it slaps down on the cold concrete. My knees ache, my chest hurts, I'm gasping for breath and we're not even halfway down. Down and down and down and down. I'm wet with sweat, my hair hanging wildly, one pearly hairslide dangling loose. I snatch it up, terrified of losing it. I think of Russell. Down and down, unable to breathe, my foot hurting so. What if they're coming after us? What will they do to us now if they catch us?

"Quick!"

"Can't go any quicker!" Nadine gasps.

"I'll never go to another step class again," Magda moans.

Down and down and down and down—and then suddenly we round the last corner and we're there, out into the courtyard, on ground level at last.

"This way!" says Magda, forging forward.

"No, wait. Keep to the edges so that if they look down they won't see us," I say.

We skirt round the sides of the tower block, legs still wobbling after all those hundreds of stairs.

"Which is the way we came in?"

"Can't remember."

"It doesn't matter. Let's just get *out*."

We scuttle on, ducking through an archway, round a corner—and then suddenly stumble upon the lager lads.

"Hey, look! It's them stupid stuck-up birds."

"There's the one that gave me the finger. I'll have her."

"I'll have the one with the big whatsits," says another, making a grab at me.

My hand flies out, hitting his face. He screams and staggers, clutching his head. His mates stare at him in astonishment.

"Quick," I say, and we start running again. We run right round the estate before we spot an exit, and then we're right out in the road at long last.

"Where now?" I gasp.

"We'll make for the nearest tube," says Magda.

"You certainly gave that guy a brilliant punch in the face, Ellie!" says Nadine.

"It wasn't a punch, it was a jab," I say, showing them my hairslide.

"You should have jabbed the guys in the flat, too!" says Magda.

"No, they could have got really really nasty," says Nadine.

"Hey, none of this seems real, does it?" I say. "I mean, we should all be watching the Claudie concert, not wandering unknown streets with mad drunk druggies in hot pursuit."

"Don't!" says Nadine, looking nervously over her shoulder. "I can't believe I could have been so stupid. Thanks so much for sticking with me, you two."

"That's what girlfriends are for," says Magda. "Hey, where on earth *are* we?"

"Maybe we're not *on* earth. Maybe we stepped into alternative time just before the Claudie concert. I mean, does it seem real that Claudie would give up her whole singing career for some inadequate boyfriend? No, in real time she's singing away and we're all singing along with her in the concert hall, right? But now we're stuck in *this* spooky time on a dead-end planet and we're going to be lost forever, meeting up with all these threatening creepy guys—"

As I'm saying these very words a couple of drunk men come lurching out a pub door and bump right into us. We all shriek.

"Hey, sorry, girls!"

"Didn't hurt you, did we?"

"Had one too many."

"A few too many."

"Where are you off to, eh?"

"Shouldn't be out late by yourselves, nice little girls like you."

We don't need to be told this. They seem relatively harmless but we don't want to take any risks. We run for it.

"I feel like I've been in a twenty-four-hour marathon aerobics class," I puff when we're right down the street and round the corner.

"Mrs. Henderson would be proud of us," Nadine gasps.

"Mrs. Henderson would be deeply *ashamed* of us because we seem to have been behaving like ninnies all night," I say, slowing down. "Look, it's daft just wandering. Let's ask someone where the tube is."

There's a late-night video shop on the corner so we dodge in and ask. The man behind the counter shakes his head.

"Sorry, girls. There's no tubes round this area. You could get a bus into Central London, but I'm not quite sure of the times. And there's been a lot of rowdy behavior on the buses when the pubs come out. I wouldn't like a daughter of mine to be on one."

"Oh help, what shall we do now?" says Magda.

"Maybe we're going to have to phone our dads," I say.

"My dad will kill me," says Nadine.

"And mine," says Magda.

"Mine too," I say. "But we can't wander the streets all night long, can we?"

"What about getting a taxi?" says Nadine. "Only I haven't got any spare cash."

"Neither have I," I say.

We both look hopefully at Magda.

"I haven't got enough for a taxi right across London and all the way home," she says. "But maybe we could get a taxi back into town to the nearest tube—and we've got our train tickets."

"What time does the last train go?" I ask anxiously.

"I don't know. But it must be quite late," says Magda.

"*We're* quite late already," says Nadine.

"We're *always* late in this alternative reality," I say.

"Shut up, Ellie! It's spooky enough without you making stuff up," says Magda.

"At least we've got each other," says Nadine, linking arms with both of us.

"Only there are replicants in this alternative world. Maybe one of *us* is a replacement!" I say. "Maybe it's you, Nadine, and you were deliberately plotting our downfall with those creeps. Or maybe it's you, Magda, and you're going to jump in a taxi by yourself and abandon Nadine and me. Or maybe it's *me*?"

"You're a one-off, Ellie. They could never program a replicant as weird and wacky as you," says Magda, and then she suddenly starts jumping up and down and waving her arms in the air.

"*I'm* wacky?" I say.

"It's a taxi!" Magda shrieks.

We all jump up and down and wave our arms in the air and it stops and we jump in.

"I'm terribly afraid we haven't got much cash on us," Magda starts.

"Well, *I'm* terribly afraid you'll have to pile straight out my cab again," says the taxi driver, but his eyes are twinkling. "You crazy girls. Right, how *much* cash—and how far do you need to go?"

Magda waves a five-pound note and Nadine and I come up with a few coins.

"That's a fair kitty," says the taxi driver, but he whistles in alarm when Magda tells him where we live. "No way, girls. I wouldn't take you that far even if you *had* the cash."

"Just to the nearest tube station?" Magda asks.

"Now you're talking. And then will you get the train from Waterloo?"

"That's what we're hoping. Do you know what time the last train goes?"

"I'm not too sure. I'd better step on it, eh, girls? You've got train tickets already, have you?"

"Oh yes," I say, and then panic when I can't find mine in my pocket.

"Help, where is it?" I say, rummaging around.

"You seem like the forgetful type," says the taxi

driver. "I couldn't help noticing you've forgotten one of your shoes!"

I wiggle my poor cold foot in its tattered tight.

"Well, I didn't exactly *forget* it," I say.

"It was all my fault," Nadine sighs.

"You girls haven't been in any real trouble, have you?" the taxi driver asks.

"Well, *nearly*," I say. "But we escaped in the nick of time."

"I don't know. You girls nowadays! How old are you? Fifteen?"

We preen and don't put him right.

"You're all allowed out so late now. And I know you think you know it all, but you act so nutty sometimes. Look at you, Miss Curly! What are you going to do? No train ticket and no cash."

"Aha!" I say, finding my ticket scrunched up at the very bottom of my purse. "Found it!"

"You're a very lucky girl," says the taxi driver, laughing.

We're all three very lucky girls because the taxi driver insists on taking us all the way to Waterloo. He stops his meter when it gets to five pounds and won't even take our spare change.

"You keep it to telephone your dads when you get off the train," he says. "I hate the thought of nice girls like you wandering the streets in the middle of the night."

We don't have to telephone our dads. You will never guess who we meet up with on the last train home! Mr. Windsor—and his girlfriend, sitting snuggled up together.

"Good Lord! Ellie. Nadine. And Magda," says Mr. Windsor.

He looks wonderful in a V-neck long-sleeved T-shirt, black jacket and black trousers—ultra-cool.

"This is Miranda," he says.

Miranda looks just as wonderful—long black hair, fantastically plaited, big brown eyes, slinky figure in tiny stripy top and black jeans.

"Hi! Are you Guy's students?" she says, giggling.

Guy!!!

We giggle too, though Magda's giggle is a little shrill.

"What are you three doing out so late?" says Mr. Windsor.

"It's a long story," I say. "We set out to go to a Claudie Coleman concert. She's this really great singer—"

"We know," says Miranda. "I'm her number one fan. Guy and I were going to the concert too. But when she canceled we trekked round half London to see if there were any other likely gigs—and ended up at this amazing *country* do, with some sad blonde doing a Tammy Wynette impersonation—"Stand by Your Man." I ask you! And they even started doing *line dancing*."

Nadine winces.

"So what did you girls do as a Claudie alternative?"

We hesitate. We shrug. Nadine looks embarrassed. Magda *already* looks embarrassed. It's down to me.

"We had a girls' night out," I say, and then I rapidly change the subject and start talking about Claudie and her songs. I can usually talk about Claudie all night long but it's pretty heavy keeping the conversation going for the entire journey, especially as Magda and Nadine remain monosyllabic.

We all get out at the same station. Mr. Windsor hesitates.

"How are you girls getting home? Is anyone meeting you?"

"We're fine," I say.

Mr. Windsor nods, but Miranda narrows her eyes.

"Does that mean you're being met or not?"

"Not," I admit.

"OK. So maybe we'd better do a little taxi service," says Mr. Windsor, sighing.

"We're not little kids," says Magda.

"Of course not," Miranda says soothingly. "But it can get a bit dodgy round the station late at night. I know I always wimp out if I've been up in town with *my* girlfriends and get Guy to pick me up from the station. So come on—*please* let us give you a lift. Especially as you've only got five shoes between the three of you."

Magda has to give in graciously. I really feel for her. It's bad enough Mr. Windsor having a girlfriend, but it's extra painful that Miranda is (a) extremely pretty and (b) extremely nice. I look her over several times to try to find *something* to be catty about tomorrow with Magda but draw a total blank. I stare at Mr. Windsor instead, hoping to see sudden signs of senility so I can convince Magda she's better off without him, but his hair looks as dark and lustrous as always and his shoulders stay square, not stooped.

He asks us all our addresses and drops us off in turn. Logically Magda should be last but he does a little detour so that she is taken home first. Maybe he's not quite as cool about everything as he makes out. He doesn't seem to have mentioned Magda's surprise visit to Miranda.

"What a sweet girl. I love her hair! But she seems ever so shy," says Miranda as Magda ducks out of the car and dives for her front door.

Nadine and I nudge each other in the dark. That's the first time Magda's ever been labeled *shy*!

"Does she say much in class, Guy?" Miranda persists.

"Oh, Magda has her moments," he says. "Right, Nadine, you're next."

Nadine gets delivered. She gives my hand one last squeeze to say sorry.

I'm left in the car with Mr. Windsor and Miranda.

"So, how do you enjoy Guy's art classes?" Miranda asks me chattily.

"Miranda!" says Mr. Windsor.

"They're great," I say truthfully.

"Really?" says Miranda. "He was *so* nervous that first week of term. What year are you, Ellie?"

"Year Nine."

"Aha! He was *particularly* scared of Year Nine. He thought you'd give him a really hard time."

"Shut up, Miranda," says Mr. Windsor.

"Oh, darling, no need to be bashful! Anyway, he came rushing home full of the joys of spring saying it had all gone splendidly after all. In fact he still raves about you Year Nine girls. You're a very talented bunch by all accounts."

"Miranda, I'm pressing my ejector seat button right this minute," says Mr. Windsor, but he's laughing.

"There's one really talented girl—she specializes in all these crazy cartoons but she's great at serious portraits too. Now, I wonder what her name is?" says Miranda.

"Who?"

They both laugh. At me.

"You must realize you're Guy's star pupil, Ellie. He's always going on about you."

"Oh wow! I mean—cool," I say, totally flustered but thrilled to bits. Star pupil! I'm twinkling all over the backseat. It's surprising the entire car isn't illuminated by my stardust.

I'm still sparkling when I let myself in at home. In spite of all the adventures of the evening I am actually back a minute before midnight, my Cinderella curfew.

I kick off my remaining shoe in the hall and try to compose myself before going into the living room. Dad's sleepily watching television and Anna is still twitching over a complicated teddy jumper with a little knitted teddy attached on a woolly string.

"Did you have a good time at your Claudie concert, Ellie?" she asks, experimenting with the dangling teddy.

I hesitate. It's simpler just to say yes. So I do.

"And Magda's dad picked you up OK after the concert?" says my dad.

"Sure," I say. "Anna, that teddy looks as if he's hung himself. He's too droopy."

"I know, I know, but I can't work out how else I can attach it. If I try to put in a pocket it'll throw the whole design out of sync and I've got to get it finished by tomorrow."

"It's mad you taking on all this work," says Dad, yawning. "Well, I'm off to bed. Come on, Anna, sort it out tomorrow, you're exhausted."

"No, I've got to fix it. Somehow," says Anna.

"Hey, what about a bit of Velcro? Then you could stick the teddy to the jumper."

"Yes! Oh, Ellie, you're a genius," says Anna, giving me a kiss.

"I'm not sure I'd go *that* far," says Dad, giving us both a big bear hug. "But you're a good girl, Ellie. I'm pleased you're being really straight with us now. No more silly lies, right?"

"Right," I say, practically swallowing my black tongue.

But it's all right. They'll never know.

Famous last words!!! There's an item in Saturday's newspaper all about Claudie Coleman and her canceled concert.

Oh help!

"Ellie!" Dad thunders.

I am in for a stormy time. I try to explain. Over and over again.

It gets me nowhere.

Magda rings. Her mum spotted the newspaper article too.

Nadine rings. Ditto *her* mum.

We were supposed to be meeting up to go shopping in the afternoon. We are not allowed. We are not allowed out anywhere apart from school for a *very* long time.

Russell rings.

"Hi, Ellie! How are you? Enjoy the concert? My dance was totally dire. I'm rather glad you weren't there, it was just so incredibly stupid and stuffy. In fact I left early because it was so boring standing there with a whole lot of other sad guys without girls. Not that I'd have wanted any of the girls who *were* there. There was no one remotely like you, Ellie. So anyway, I got home early, like I said, and my dad was pleased and said he's glad I'm behaving like a responsible human being at last—so I'm not grounded anymore. We can go out on our first proper date. Tonight! Remember I said I knew where I wanted to go? How about the seven-thirty showing of *Girls Out Even Later*? It's still on at the Rio."

"There's just one problem, Russell."

"Don't worry about it being scary. I'll hold your hand tight, I promise. Everyone says *Girls Out*

Even Later is a really great film. Well, not great art, just great fun."

"Russell—"

"But don't worry. We don't have to see it if you really think it might upset you. We'll go anywhere you want."

"I can't go to *Girls Out Even Later*. I can't go out late myself. Or early. Oh Russell, I'm in big trouble. *I'm* not allowed out for ages now."

I explain. Russell listens. Groans. Tells me off for taking crazy risks. Moans that we can't go out after all.

"So it's back to secret after-school trysts in Mc-Donald's?" he says.

"It looks like it."

"Ah well. I suppose it can't be helped. We'll have our big night out *one* day, right?"

"You bet."

"Good. Because you mean a lot to me, Ellie." There's a little pause. I hear him swallow. "Ellie . . . I love you."

I swallow too. I glance around quickly to make sure Eggs isn't lurking.

"I love you, too," I whisper, and then I put the phone down.

I pick it up again. Who shall I phone first, Magda or Nadine? I can't wait to tell them what Russell's just said!

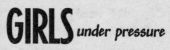